1

THE FUNERAL

It felt kind of strange to be sharing a joke at a funeral, but Mavis Johns had not registered high on the affection meter of many of the people who had known her. In fact, even her sister, Delores, was having a chuckle with one of the waiters manning the heavily loaded drinks table.

Jessica Lemond started as her father, Benjamin, came up behind her, tapping her on the shoulder. 'Do you think we should get him home soon?'

'Who?'

Benjamin poked a finger back over his shoulder. 'Dad. Your grandpa. He's over there trying to pick up the undertaker.'

'Literally pick up?'

Benjamin winced as though the thought of saying the words out loud left a funny taste in his mouth. 'No ... he's single again, now, isn't he? He's on the pull.'

'Dad, he's ninety-two.'

'Exactly. Not much time left. And with Mavis out of

the way, he's got the keys to the cheque book back again hasn't he?'

'You don't really think…?'

Benjamin patted her gently on the shoulder again, as he might have once done when she was five, shortly before a piano recital or a school play. She considered reminding him she was twenty-nine, and the owner of her own business, albeit one of which he'd never approved, nor shown any interest.

'Be a love and go play gooseberry, won't you? We'll either end up with another funeral or another marriage on our hands, and to be honest, it really is about time he put his feet up.'

'Can't we just let him go out with a bang?'

'What?'

Jessica slapped a hand over her mouth. 'Oh, I didn't mean literally with a … oh, Jesus.'

'Don't use the Lord's name in vain, dear,' said her mother, Emelia, swanning over and putting an arm around Jessica's shoulders. Wearing a floral dress which might have been more appropriate at a summer fair, Emelia Lemond had never bothered to hide her dislike for her father-in-law's third wife. 'Great party, isn't it? I can't wait for the karaoke.'

'I'll be long gone by then, I hope,' Jessica said. 'I have a booking.'

'Oh, God, he's slipping her his number,' Benjamin said.

'At least that's all he's slipping her,' Emelia said. 'The dirty old sod. And you can pack it in with the Gods and Jesuses as well.'

'What?' Benjamin frowned, then let out a huff. He gave Jessica a little shove in the back. 'Go on, love, quick. Save that poor woman from my letch of a father. Or at the very least, save us from having to hear all about his conquest at Sunday lunch next week.'

Jessica found herself hobbling on uncomfortable heels across the dancefloor, leaving her parents to swing into a jive as the music continued its inappropriate joviality. Grandpa, propped up on a walking frame, was leaning over the undertaker, a stern, masculine woman in her early fifties who wore a man's suit over a black frilled blouse.

'You have YouTube, don't you?' he was saying, his voice containing a fluttery waver that sounded as though he could pass out at any moment. 'All my best gags are on there. Why did my brother lose his job in a lemon factory? Because he couldn't concentrate.'

The undertaker laughed with such sudden ferocity that Jessica stumbled, catching the heel of her shoe in a crack in the floor tiles at the same moment. She twisted, back-ending the trestle table just at the moment the undertaker thumped the tabletop hard enough to make a large bowl of trifle shudder. Jessica's bum caught the lip, and while she didn't see the sudden cascade of sponge, jelly, and whipped cream, she felt it soaking the back of her dress, gunk running down over her hips and thighs.

She closed her eyes. When she opened them, Grandpa was staring at her with an incredulous look on his face. 'Oh. What happened to you, love? A party for one, is it? Hang on, I'll just get my spoon.'

If there was a joke buried in his words somewhere, it was lost on Jessica. The undertaker, however, broke into another horrifying guffaw. Jessica closed her eyes, for once feeling envious of Mavis, now entirely reduced to dust.

'You didn't have to drink all of the punch, dear,' Emilia

said, taking a brief break from the dancefloor to check on her daughter, sitting on a sofa chair against the wall of the community centre, an empty plastic beaker lolling in her hand.

'I didn't,' Jessica said, aware she was slurring. 'I tried to, but Grandpa siphoned what was left into a flask to take home.'

'Oh, he's left, has he?'

'With the undertaker, about half an hour ago. I saw them getting into a taxi.'

Emilia laughed. 'Well, at least she's an appropriate person to be on hand if he overexerts himself.'

'Mum, stop! That's disgusting.'

Emilia, however, was on a roll. 'That randy old sod. At his wife's funeral too. What a way to celebrate finally being rid of that witch, by banging the undertaker.'

'Please, Mum,' Jessica said, covering her ears. 'I want this nightmare to end.'

'Didn't you have to go to work tonight? Cleaning someone's pipes or something?'

Jessica groaned. 'I'm a plumber. Can you please quit the stupid jokes? This is supposed to be a funeral.'

'Ah, but what a funeral. Who could possibly have expected that sow to fall off a ladder at her age? She was what, forty-five?'

'Forty-seven.'

'And a yoga instructor, a climbing teacher, and what else was it?'

'A professional skydiver. She presented some documentary or other on cable.'

'So unexpected, wasn't it? And look at him … her ashes are still warm to the touch and he's out reliving his youth.' Emilia leaned close, a conspiratorial grin on her face. 'Your father won't hear a word of it, but between you and me, do you think he knocked her off?'

As though on cue, a flashing blue light appeared outside the window. Jessica stood up and peered outside, just in time to see three police cars pulling into the community centre car park.

Emelia was still grinning. 'Told you, didn't I?'

2

FUGITIVE

'NO WORK TONIGHT, LEMONS?' DOREEN SAID, appearing out of her bedroom with a crunched can of Worthington Bitter in her hand. She went to the sink, up-ended it to let a dribble of froth run out, then left it—unwashed—on the worktop before retrieving another from the fridge. 'It's Arsenal versus West Ham at seven-thirty. Are you likely to go out?'

Jessica, sitting at their shared dining room table with a tradesman's magazine open in front of her and a coffee close at hand, suppressed a sigh. 'I wasn't planning to, but I suppose I could pop down to the Coco Lounge for a bit.'

'Seriously?'

Jessica felt herself blushing. 'Well, you don't want me here, do you?'

'Not unless you're into the game. It kind of sucks to watch with someone who's not up for it.' Doreen, Jessica's lodger, a hardcore lesbian and football fan, who worked as a hairdresser and also happened to be a casual bully, planted powerful fists on hips honed at combat-fit classes, and pouted.

'But even so, the Coco Lounge? You're going to go in there alone? You might as well just wear a green t-shirt and walk up and down the high street flashing your boobs at cars.'

Jessica was at a loss for words. 'Well, what would you suggest?'

'Couldn't you just stay in your room? Read a book or something?'

'It's my flat.'

Doreen raised an eyebrow and Jessica knew she'd crossed the line. 'So, you're saying I'm not wanted? Would you like me to pack my bags?'

Jessica flapped a hand, feeling backed into a corner. Whatever she said was likely to leave her trailing in one way or another. Either she ruined Doreen's football night by staying in, or she ruined Doreen's cred by going to a couples bar alone.

'I didn't mean it like that. I'm sorry. Perhaps I'll go to the supermarket or something.'

Doreen's eyes lit up. 'Really? I know it's a bit of a walk, but if you go down to the LIDL there's a two-for-one on John Smiths. Mick and Phil are coming round in a bit so we wouldn't mind if you dropped them off at half-time. We'll probably be dry by then.'

Jessica opened her mouth to say something, but all sense of confrontation was gone. 'Sure. No problem.'

Doreen grinned. 'You know Mick's single, don't you? He dumped that Kathleen bird last month. Apparently he caught her watching Tottenham. I mean, come on. Gunners for life. She should have known better.'

'He's not really my type—'

Doreen's face hardened again. 'Don't you start with that fat-shaming rubbish. He's well-built, that's all. Nothing wrong with that. Unless you're saying you don't like bigger people?' Doreen looked ready for a scrap. 'Who else don't you like?'

Jessica stood up quickly. 'I'll go and get your beer,' she said. 'And if I can't think of anything else to do, I'll just wander the streets for a bit until the game's over. It's not that cold.'

Doreen grinned. 'You're the best, Lemons. I knew I was doing the right thing when I agreed to a flat share.'

Agreed to rent a room in my flat, Jessica forced herself not to say. *You're my lodger. You rent one room, and you pay under the going rate for it. And in less than six months you've made me just about ready to pack a bag and run.*

As she headed for the door, taking her jacket off the back of a chair, she heard Doreen switching on the TV to the match buildup. Then, to Jessica's utter revulsion, she heard the sound of the sofa springs stretching to their max.

Doreen was jumping up and down.

It was freezing outside, as might have been expected for mid-November. All the news programs were claiming a monster winter this year, a dump of snowfall unheard of in living memory. The very thought of it sent shivers down Jessica's spine, and not just because she wasn't a fan of the horribly cold and wet stuff. It meant a slew of cracked pipes which would keep her busy right over the holiday season. As a plumber who specialised in unsociable work hours for people who couldn't arrange to be home during the day, she ought to be pleased, but she had been looking forward to over-eating, getting drunk, and doing all the things everyone else got to do. While crawling under a porch at midnight to inspect a burst pipe was fine during

8

the summer months, the prospect was a lot bleaker during winter.

And this Christmas season was a special one, too. Turning thirty in January, it was her last as a young woman. After January, she was officially middle-aged. 'Washed-up,' as Doreen—still only twenty-six—liked to put it. 'Might as well start playing for the other team,' her lodger was fond of saying. 'I'm not saying we have lower standards, but you're not likely to get much of a boyfriend now, are you?'

She walked up the high street, past the Tesco where she preferred to shop, all the way down to the LIDL on the edge of the town centre, just before her Bristol suburb gave itself over to bland new housing estates. She looked up at the geometric rows of boring houses, most of which had perfect water systems which wouldn't require her services until she was due to retire, and wondered whether they'd only added street signs to stop people getting lost.

She picked up Doreen's beer, grumbling under her breath for having forgotten to bring her own bag and having to buy one instead, then made her way back up the high street, past several small shops which already had Christmas decorations displayed in the windows, fairy lights glittering brightly against backdrops of snowy winter scenes, plastic Father Christmases, nodding wire-framed reindeer, and electric candles in the shape of elves—all of which appeared of the same tribe; a likely result of Pound Stretcher further up the street having a sale on last year's stock.

The little paper craft shop which had long been Jessica's favourite—not because she ever bought any paper crafts, but because it was so quaint and unique—had a new sign up in the window.

OUR LAST CHRISTMAS
Get your paper crafts now
Closing December 31st
Thanks for 30 years of business!

Something about it made Jessica sad, and she reached into her pocket for her phone, needing the comfort of social media, or perhaps even a call to someone she knew. Instead, there was a missed call from Dad. She picked it up to reply, just as her battery died.

The thought of using a phone box made her grimace, but by now Doreen and her meathead mates would have taken over her flat to watch the game. Ignoring the one outside the Wetherspoon's pub which no doubt doubled down as a urinal, she headed up the street, past her own road, to the small park at the end. A pair of phone boxes stood next to the park gates, so she squeezed into one and pulled a handful of change out of her pocket.

'Jess, is that you?' came Benjamin's voice. 'What happened? Are you in hospital or something? A car accident?'

'My phone battery died. What's up? Your message said to call you urgently. Have they found Grandpa yet?'

She could almost hear Dad umming on the other end of the line, wondering what to say. With Grandpa having gone on the run from police and been missing for two weeks now, both Jessica and her mum were convinced Mavis's death had been murder. Doreen was certain old Ernest Lemond, a famous TV comedian from the nineteen-fifties, was set to kill again. Dad, however, wouldn't hear of it. While Mavis had been a tyrant, a fitness freak with a penchant for spending her elderly husband's money, Grandpa, in his advanced years, had held her in something like affection, even if the rest of the family despised her. And in any case, Mavis had outweighed him by twenty kilograms. There was no way he could have pushed her off that ladder.

'No … the police haven't found him.'

'Okay. Is that good or bad?'

'It depends on how you look at it. However, a postcard arrived yesterday.'

'A postcard?'

'Yes. From Scotland.'

Jessica lifted an eyebrow, her genetically inherited sense of humour unable to miss the opportunity for a bad joke. 'Really?' she said. 'I didn't know you and Scotland were such good friends.'

'Jess … you'd put the old man into his grave with something as poor as that,' Benjamin said, squeezing out a reluctant laugh. 'From your grandfather in Scotland.'

'What's he doing there?'

'Evading the police. And he told me he's got a job over the Christmas season as the in-house comedian at a ski lodge.'

'Do they have ski lodges in Scotland? I didn't realise they had that much snow.'

'Obviously his postcard didn't contain much detail, but it seems they must do. Especially if they're in a position to hire a professional comedian, even if he is ninety-two.'

'Well, good luck to him.'

Dad sighed, and Jessica knew his own punchline was coming. 'Look. You know your mother and me have that cruise booked in the Fjords through December. We really don't have time to go rushing off to Scotland to bring Grandpa to justice. However, I was wondering….'

Jessica tapped the phone receiver. 'Come on, Dad, I've only got one more quid. I can't go and charge my phone because Doreen's mates are round and one of them might steal it. Let's hear it. What do you want me to do?'

'I was wondering if you could go up there and, well, just check on him? You don't have to force him to turn himself in, but just make sure he's all right. He is ninety-two, after all, and he is my father. You'd do it for me, wouldn't you?'

'Bring you to justice if you knocked off Mum?' Jessica smirked. 'Of course I would.'

'Do you think you could go, then?'

'Dad, I have to work … I need to find somewhere else to live—'

'Really?'

'Doreen's kind of outstayed her welcome.'

'Doreen? That lovely girl you've got staying with you?'

Jessica rolled her eyes. Doreen had done a number on her parents on the only time they'd met. Dad now wouldn't hear a bad word about her.

'I'm afraid we have a couple of … personality clashes,' Jessica said. 'And she really likes the flat, so it looks like I'll have to find somewhere else. I was kind of counting on the Christmas rush to fund it.'

Dad was silent for a few seconds, and Jessica sensed a guilt trip coming. Of course, they wouldn't change their plans, but she was expected to change hers.

'He's ninety-two,' Dad said quietly. 'He could be dead by this time next year, or at best, behind bars. I had a, um, lifetime of him, but you … well, you did miss out a bit when you were young.'

'He was doing a residency in Vegas. I could hardly expect him to show up on my birthdays with a Barbie and a card.'

'No, of course not. So now's your chance to get a bit of quality time with him.'

Jessica sighed. Dad wasn't about to relent. Even if she missed the Christmas rush, it might be nice just to escape Doreen for a while. Plus, if this ski lodge had given Grandpa a job, it might give her one, too. Especially if the coming winter was as bad as the weather forecasts were predicting.

'Okay, tell me the name of the place and I'll look it up online. No promises, though.'

'Sure. Hang on a minute.'

Jessica heard the rustle of papers as her dad searched for Grandpa's postcard.

'Ah, here it is. Are you ready? Do you have a pen?'

'I have a brain that's still young.'

'No need to be sarcastic. Right, I've got the name now. Oh, isn't it quaint.' Dad gave a little chuckle, and Jessica was tempted to just hang up and walk away.

'Dad?'

'Snowflake Lodge.'

3

SECOND THOUGHTS

'You've got some Shake n' Vac under the sink, haven't you? Mick dropped a can of Guinness on the carpet.'

Jessica gave a resigned sigh. 'And you didn't notice until it had soaked right through?'

Doreen rolled her eyes. 'We were celebrating a goal. What is this? Prison?'

For one of us, at least, Jessica didn't say. While planting a right hook on Doreen's jutting chin might have made her feel better, she settled for a far more passive, 'But it's a cream carpet. If I wanted to sell, I'd have to replace it now.'

Doreen's eyes hardened again. 'So now you're going to sell, is it? You're going to make me homeless?' She shook her head. 'Talk about driving the knife in. Do you know what I've been through?'

Jessica winced, fearful that Doreen would start to tell her. In truth, a couple of not-particularly-dramatic breakups was about as hardcore as Doreen's life had gotten.

'I'm not going to sell. I was speaking hypothetically.'

Doreen's face relaxed. 'Don't worry, it's only a little stain. And if it doesn't come out, they've got some nice little foot rug things in LIDL. Didn't you notice them last night?'

'I was too busy in the booze aisle.'

'I've been worried about your drinking issues for a while. Seriously.'

Jessica grimaced. 'Thanks for your concern. Look, I'll sort it out tonight. I have to go to work.'

'Now? But it's only lunchtime. Don't you usually work nights? I wanted to ask you about my radiator. It's been making a funny noise.'

'It's fine. It's just kind of waking up because it hasn't been used since last winter. It's not a problem.'

'I hope not. You charge me enough rent as it is without leaving me without decent heating. There's nothing to me. I'd be dead by Christmas. Oh, by the way, Mick left you this.'

She stuffed a piece of paper into Jessica's hand. Jessica unfolded it and squinted at the squiggles written diagonally across a piece of her own notepaper.

'What's this?'

'It's his number. I told him you'd been single for ages and since you were coming up for thirty you might be up for a sympathy shag.'

Jessica was too stunned to speak. She gave a dumb nod, then folded the paper and stuffed it into her pocket.

'He's alright, Mick, once you've had a few,' Doreen said. 'I mean, objectively speaking. I wouldn't know. Once he hits that five-pint mark he starts to get a bit rowdy, but maybe that's your thing.'

'Maybe,' Jessica said, voice hollow, wishing the

Guinness had done enough damage to make the floor open up and swallow her. 'I have to go.'

Doreen was still talking, her words systematically eradicating Jessica's confidence, sense of self-worth, and faith in humanity, one abrasive swipe at a time. Jessica, letting her vision glaze over, turned to the door, grabbed her bag on autopilot, and made her escape.

'You won't forget to check the radiator, will you, Lemons?' was the last thing she heard as the door slammed behind her. Then she was running, running down the stairs and out on to the street.

She took a deep breath of chilly November air. Things couldn't possibly get worse. Her Grandpa was on the run from the police, and her lodger was slowly evicting her. Only if—

A car came roaring past, swerving too close to the curb. From somewhere behind it came the sound of a police siren, then the car was gone, but not before hitting a muck-filed pothole turned into gunk by last night's rain. Jessica stared in horror at the brown stain on her dress. At least she had her work clothes with her … her work clothes that were hanging up to dry on her balcony.

Life couldn't possibly … better hold that thought.

Kirsten was waiting outside the Coco Lounge, her bag held protectively across her chest, a worried look on her face as her eyes darted around, perhaps expecting someone to jump out and scream 'Boo!' at any given moment. Jessica gave her a reassuring wave as she came around the corner, then waved Kirsten back as her government trainee started forward to meet her in the middle of the street.

'Good morning, Miss Lemond,' Kirsten said, making Jessica inwardly groan.

'Hi, Kirsten. You could have gone in and got a table, you know.'

Kirsten looked distraught. 'I'm sorry, I thought, just, well, you might have wanted to go somewhere else, or perhaps—'

'No, no, I asked to meet you here because we always meet here on a Wednesday.'

'I do apologise—'

'It's okay. Come on, let's get inside before we freeze to death.'

'Do you think I'm appropriately dressed for today's lesson?' Kirsten asked, tugging at the jacket she wore, the jacket that she had worn every single time Jessica had seen her since she had agreed to a government subsidized program to take on a trainee.

'I think you'll do just fine. It's only theory again today, I'm afraid.'

They went inside. During the day, the Coco Lounge was a shadow of its thumping evening self. Much preferable in many ways, its quaint Mexican-styled décor could be seen without a throng of drinking people in the way, and the tables were clean and neatly arranged. They took the same table they always did, in the window with a view of the high street outside.

Jessica ordered a latte as she always did, while Kirsten pored over the menu like she always did, before going for an iced lemon tea, as she always did. Then, as she always did, she offered to pay, and Jessica had to remind her—as she always did—that she claimed it on government program expenses, and that Kirsten was welcome to order something more expensive, or even a chocolate brownie, if she wanted, which she never did.

Sometimes, having a trainee was almost as exhausting as living with Doreen.

'Today we'll be going over the various ways to unblock an old toilet system built before the nineteen-thirties,' Jessica said, leaning forward. Kirsten, whom Jessica was certain was more deserving of a vocation in the library or perhaps underground filing system world, peered over the top of her glasses at the file in Jessica's hands. The secrets of the world it was not, but Kirsten looked as though an Egyptian tomb was about to be opened for the first time.

'When you work unusual hours like we do, you get a lot of calls from museums and other historical public buildings who don't want to disrupt the flow of customers. While there are all sorts of government regulations regarding plumbing, many of these places have cut corners or simply not bothered to upgrade their systems. And when a blockage happens … chaos reigns. And that's where we come in.'

'Right.' Kirsten was nodding her head as though listening to a Bond villain explain a master plan. Jessica wondered just how much of her grandfather's genes she'd taken on when she found herself playing up to Kirsten's adulation a little.

'This,' she said, pulling something out of her bag and holding it up, 'is a u-bend.'

She waited for Kirsten to say, 'The Holy Grail,' but unfortunately her plumbing fantasy wasn't translating. As a waiter brought their drinks and gave Jessica a funny look, Kirsten just nodded again, and said, 'I see.'

Not for the first time—more like the hundredth—Jessica was tempted to ask whether Kirsten really wanted to be a plumber. In truth, she had herself fallen into the profession, and her particular take on it, more or less by chance, while sitting in a café browsing through a local college pamphlet one day, while at the adjacent table a pair of well-to-do old ladies were complaining that they could never find someone to come out when their busy schedules required it.

'Just out of interest,' she found herself saying as she sipped the froth off the top of her latte, 'when was it you realised that you wanted a career in the water pipe maintenance field?'

For the first time Kirsten's face lit up beyond pure concentration. 'When I read your article in Tradesman,' she said. 'And the pictures of you … you looked so … cool.'

Jessica suppressed a grimace. The photography team had done a number on her, performing a glamorous shoot which had little connection to the nuts and bolts of the article. Doreen had laughed about it for days, but one of the reasons Jessica had taken on a trainee was because she had begun receiving dozens of daily calls from older single men with piping issues. After one frightful occasion when she had turned up to find her client still in a dressing gown, she had decided she needed some cavalry. Kirsten, with her bookish look and seeming obliviousness to even the most blatant innuendo, had been a perfect solution.

'I have a few questions,' Kirsten said.

'Sure.'

'Firstly, would it be a good idea to go for my NVQ in plastering now, or do you think it's better to hire outside help when renovation work is required in order to build up a network of contacts while also helping the wider tradesman community?'

With Kirsten having read the lengthy handwritten question off a sheet of paper without any kind of tonal stress, Jessica was left momentarily speechless.

'Um, well, I think you should do what you think is best,' she said at last.

'Right.' Kirsten scribbled down a note. 'And another question: do you think that in situations of dry wall degradation—'

Jessica held up a hand. 'Let's get going,' she said, downing the rest of her latte, pausing briefly to make sure she didn't choke, and then quickly standing up. 'We should get to our first appointment.'

'Can I continue to ask questions in the van?'

'Sure,' Jessica said, hoping the traffic wouldn't hold them up too long.

Their afternoon appointment finished just before three. They had another booking at eight p.m. at an old house on the outskirts of the city which was being used as a TV drama location. Apparently, a crew party had gotten a bit rowdy and someone had flushed a handful of historic coins down the toilet. Stuck somewhere in the ancient pipe, the producers were keen to get it fixed before the house owners or the rest of the cast found out. With a few hours to kill, however, Jessica couldn't face going home, so instead she dropped Kirsten off outside the Waterstones bookshop in the town centre and then headed over to her parents' place in Clifton.

She found her mother packing a suitcase in the front room.

'Dear, do you think the green fake fur or the red fake fur?'

Jessica shrugged. 'How cold are the fjords likely to be in December? Perhaps you should take both.'

Emilia patted her on the arm. 'What a grand idea. Of

course. I'll have to pay for extra baggage, but it's more about the convenience than the cost, isn't it?'

Jessica couldn't help but smile. 'Perhaps you should hire a little Christmas elf to help you carry it?'

'Do you think I could order one online?' Emilia said, without either batting an eyelid or looking up. 'I imagine they'll be busy around this time of year.'

Jessica gave a little sigh and shrugged. 'Oh, I'm sure you could.'

'Your father's in the garden,' Emilia said, the hint so lacking subtlety that had it come with a glowing neon sign it couldn't have been more obvious. 'He's worried about his seed beds in the frost. Why don't you go and reassure him? I'll just finish up here, then we'll have afternoon tea.'

'Sure, sounds nice.'

Jessica looked around as she headed out of the living room and down the hall to the wide kitchen. Three floors of Bristol's most elegant Edwardian architecture, high ceilings and airy, well-lit rooms, all renovated and modernised in exactly the way her parents had wanted. And every single corner of it paid for by Grandpa's fortune.

Dad was where Mum had said, down by the back of their long, leafy garden, standing by a freshly dug flowerbed that had probably been turned over by Reg, the gardener, rather than Dad, who preferred to inspect rather than get his hands dirty. To Jessica's surprise, he was wearing a pair of gardening gloves, standing with his hands on his hips, an empty wheelbarrow beside him.

'Hi, Dad, what are you doing?'

'Oh, hello, love. Great to see you. I was just wondering whether to cover this over with a sheet to keep the leaves off, or just leave it.'

Jessica just shrugged. 'A big decision, I'm sure.'

'Well, once we're on that ship there will be a lot of distractions. I've told Reg to just do as he sees fit, but I like to be around just in case.'

'Sure, Dad.'

Benjamin looked up. 'Have you thought any more about what I asked you?'

'You mean, rushing off to Scotland to bring my fugitive grandfather to justice?'

'I got another postcard the other day,' Benjamin said. 'Apparently he's got a new girlfriend. Some floozy he met on Tinder. Do you think he'll marry her? That could really screw the inheritance. It was a lucky escape with Mavis, don't you know.'

Jessica grimaced. 'You know, not everything in life is about Grandpa's money—'

'It's your inheritance too.'

Before Jessica could construct a reply that would both appease her father while emphasising that she had no intention of spending her life living off her grandfather's fortune in the same way her parents did, Emilia appeared on the back porch with a tray of tea and biscuits.

'Oh, Benjamin! Jessica! I've finished packing … I think. How about a little celebration?'

'Oh, delightful,' Benjamin said. 'Did you go with the yellow jacket in the end?'

Emilia's face darkened. 'The yellow? You think I should go with the yellow?'

'I was just thinking about the matinees, dear,' Benjamin said. 'It would so fit with the décor we saw in those photographs.'

Emilia almost dropped the tray. 'I'd better go and check,' she said, rushing back into the house.

Benjamin pulled off his gloves. 'Okay, tea time. I'm famished. I wonder what Dillingtons has delivered this time? They do the best afternoon tea deliveries. You really should think about a subscription.'

Jessica could only imagine what Doreen would think of her parents' subscription to an afternoon tea delivery service. She'd probably ask for a reduction on the rent.

'Actually, Dad, I'd better be off,' Jessica said. 'I just stopped by to see how you were getting on. I have a job this evening.'

Benjamin gave her shoulder a gentle squeeze. 'Jess … you know you don't have to work, don't you? And such a dirty profession. If you really insist on having a job, couldn't you be a secretary or something?'

Jessica needed to leave before she screamed loud enough to have the neighbours calling the police. She eased away from Dad and started up the path.

'If I don't see you before, have a good cruise,' she said.

'Think about what I said,' Benjamin said, frowning at the flowerbed as though he had caught it playing pranks in the night. 'I'm so worried about Grandpa, I really wish you'd go up and check on him. Go on, just take December off. It won't hurt. The estate will spot you if you need any money.'

Jessica cringed at the thought. 'I don't want to let my clients down.'

'Well, do as you will. But if you decide not to go, could you be a love and stop in every couple of days just to check on the house and make sure Reg doesn't do anything too dramatic to my garden?'

Jessica held her breath, wondering how long she would need to do it before she passed out. The old Catch 22. *Damned if I do, damned if I don't.*

'I'd better be going, Dad,' she said, even as from somewhere inside the house came Emilia's piercing cry, 'Or do you think the blue sash would be better?'

4

IDEAS

THE SMELL OF CURRY MET JESSICA AS SOON AS SHE opened the front door of her building and stepped in out of the cold. She had barely shaken her umbrella off on the mat when the nearest downstairs flat door opened and old Mrs. Giddons, who lived directly underneath Jessica's flat, stepped out, a rolling pin in her hand to show she meant business.

'Any chance you could go easy on the spices up there?' she growled, hitting the rolling pin into her palm, the curlers in her hair shaking with each strike like the bristles on an angry porcupine. 'You're causing my windows to steam up. I've told you about this before. I won't stand for it. Every Wednesday I have to put up with this stink, and I've barely aired it out before the next week rolls around.'

'It's my lodger, Doreen,' Jessica said, giving Mrs. Giddons her best there's-nothing-I-can-do expression. 'She has curry night every Wednesday.'

'How about kicking her out on the street?'

'It's a long-term agreement,' Jessica said, certain that if she even tried, Doreen would be 'up for a scrap over it'.

'I'll see if I can get her to cook something a little milder next week. A korma, perhaps?'

'You've got Madras Kitchen a stone's throw down the street,' Mrs. Giddons snapped. 'Tell her to take it on the road.'

'She got barred,' Jessica said. 'For fighting. She threw a chair at a skinhead who refused to down a cup of chili sauce.'

'Just sort it out,' Mrs. Giddons said. 'I'm a patient woman, Lemons, but even my supply of patience is running out.'

As she stomped back inside, Jessica winced at her use of her hated school nickname. It was catching. Doreen had adopted it after her father had mentioned it 'as a joke' during their one and only meeting. And now her lodger's propensity to throw it around like a tennis ball at a playground game of bucks was starting to turn her carefully cultivated adult life into the same nightmare she had endured at school.

With a resigned shrug, she headed upstairs. The smell was thicker here, and when she opened her door, the stench of spice was so strong it made her cough. The sound of WWE—Doreen's second favorite sport after football—came through the open door to the living room, followed by a bellow of 'Ooh! Tombstone! Dor! Dor? You've got to see this!'

Afraid of what she might see, Jessica peered into the kitchen. Doreen, wearing an Arsenal apron, turned around, a wooden spoon in her hand dripping thick red sauce all over the lino.

'Christ, you scared me. Can't you knock?'

'It's my flat—'

'And you said you were working tonight. Look, I've only made enough for the three of us.'

The vat of curry cooking on the stove was big enough to feed half the street. Six fresh naan stood in a stack, while a pan of cooked rice had overflowed onto the worktop.

'It's okay. I'll get something in a bit.'

Doreen planted her hands on her hips. 'You said you were working.'

'They cancelled—'

'Look, if you really have to, I can spot you a bit. There's not much rice so you might want to run down the chippy. If you do, grab us a couple of larges.'

'Um, I—'

'And we're low on booze—'

'No.'

'What?'

'I said no.'

Doreen frowned. As her face hardened, Jessica wondered what she had just said. The single word that had defined protests for millennia had slipped out like a mouse escaping from a hungry cat, making a break for it before she even knew it was happening.

'Are you starting on me?' Doreen said, putting the spoon down with a snap that splashed curry across the floral paper on the back wall. 'Because if you are—'

'All right, Jess,' came a walrus-like bellow from behind her. Jessica turned to see Mick, almost as wide as he was tall, his head like a softened football squashing neckless down on shoulders as wide and sloping as Glastonbury Tor. Beady eyes squinted at her.

'Hey, Mick. All right?'

'Yeah, you?'

'Yeah.'

'Yeah.'

Doreen was still glaring at her. Jessica grimaced, then rubbed her head. 'I'm not feeling well today, that's all. I think I have a cold coming on, and I don't want to go back out, otherwise I would. I think I'll get an early night.' She thought about asking them to turn down the TV, but it was never going to happen. From over Mick's shoulder came a cry of 'Bang! Piledriver!'

Doreen smiled. 'You should have just said. There's some bread left if you want some toast later. Just give me a shout and I'll get it out of the bread bin for you.'

'Thanks, Dor.'

'You take it easy. You work too much.'

'Yeah, I do.'

Doreen continued to stare at her, which Jessica took as her cue to make herself scarce. Wishing good night to Mick, she headed into her bedroom and closed the door.

Thankfully, the door had been closed, so the smell of Doreen's massive pan of vindaloo was subtle at best. She dropped her bag in a corner, kicked off her shoes, and then slumped down on her bed, wondering whether she would pluck up the courage to go back out again, or whether an evening of hunger was preferable to negotiating the minefield that was Doreen all over again.

From the other side of the door came a sudden elongated howl: 'Hounds .... of Justice!', which Jessica hoped was a wrestling group and not a form of retribution heading her way for the ignominy of disturbing their curry night. There was no chance she would be able to sleep nor concentrate on a book, so she pulled out her phone and did the usual time-wasting stuff, browsing social media she had no interest in, watching boring videos, looking for a few articles on BBC which she hadn't either already read or scrolled past. Only when she found herself watching a short video about frozen ice caves in Siberia, did she remember the name of the place to which her grandfather had apparently fled.

Snowflake Lodge.

It sounded like some kind of fairytale palace, perhaps where you could meet Santa Claus at Alton Towers or Thorpe Park during the Christmas season. She had little hope that the reality would live up to its name, but when she put the name into the search box the image results made her gasp.

Set on a forested hillside, surrounded by snowcapped mountains and with a view of the Scottish moors, it looked like something you'd find in Lapland or Switzerland, rather than in the wilds of Scotland.

The homepage was displaying a Christmas season itinerary, which involved numerous Christmas-themed events such as sleigh rides, carol singing, an audience with Father Christmas, as well as cookery and craft classes, cabaret and comedy nights—featuring a "very special guest", and even an interactive Christmas theatre in which guests could participate. Set against a peaceful countryside backdrop with dozens of nature trails accessible even during the winter, it was a perfect place for a seasonal getaway.

Jessica found herself clicking on the booking button.

Fully booked until February.

She sighed. That was the end of that, then. Perhaps it might be better to move back into her parents' place as a de facto caretaker over the Christmas season. Last year, Doreen's Christmas party had turned into a huge punch up, with the police getting called and two of Doreen's friends spending Christmas night in the slammer. Jessica had had to replace the living room carpet, buy a new TV, and repair a hole in the wall where someone had impaled an ornamental sword. Doreen had still been chuckling about it months later.

She was about to venture out to the toilet when she

happened on a thought. Grandpa hadn't gone there to stay; he was apparently working there. Perhaps he needed an assistant?

Jessica logged back on to the website and found a JOB OPPORTUNITIES listing at the bottom. There were a couple for kitchen staff, and one for a cabaret singer which she winced at. But there, at the very bottom was something that made her heart flutter with possibilities.

PERSON REQUIRED FOR
PLUMBING AND GENERAL MAINTENANCE
Winter season only
Must be prepared to work unsociable hours
Full room and board included
Salary negotiable

Jessica's fingers were trembling so much she had to fill out the online application twice before she could manage it without typos. Then, clicking SEND, she sat back, heart thundering. Perhaps she could escape this mayhem after all.

Just as she was thinking of perhaps running out and getting a glass of wine to celebrate, she heard a roar from the other room:

'Hold it in, Mick! Hold it! No, don't … don't … ahhhhhhh!'

She felt the thud as something hit the other side of her bedroom wall, curry or beer or perhaps some combination of both. She closed her eyes, wishing that at least this part of her life could only be a bad dream.

5

INVESTIGATIONS PENDING

THE NEXT MORNING, A TRAINSPOTTING POSTER HAD appeared on the wall behind the living room sofa. Doreen was watching Breakfast TV with a bowl of cornflakes on her lap, sitting on the sofa, which had been pushed tight against the wall and now had a throw blanket over it. Jessica must have glanced in the wrong direction, because without saying anything, Doreen turned to her, put her remaining cornflakes down on the coffee table hard enough to make a splash, looked up, and said: 'What? I thought it looked a bit dull in here, that's all.'

Jessica had never been to university, but remembered the house she had shared during vocational college well enough. There had been some fun times, but the décor had never impressed. She'd once asked one of her housemates if he knew who Che Guevara was, having hung his imposingly large portrait over their shared TV. Her housemate had shrugged and told her he'd played bass in Nirvana.

'It's fine,' she said.

'I'm just concerned that you're taking this thirty stuff

too seriously,' Doreen said. 'I mean, who cares if you haven't got a boyfriend or a decent job? It's not like your life is going to end when you turn the big three-oh. Obviously you won't be able to go on any eighteen-thirties holidays without looking like a sugar mama or a pervert, but there's other stuff you can do, like go on those archeological holidays to like Hadrian's Wall or something. It's not all bad.'

'No,' Jessica said.

'So where are you going?'

'To the kitchen. To get breakfast.'

Doreen cleared her throat. 'The pipe's blocked.'

Jessica took a deep breath. 'Is it? Why?'

'Phil wasn't feeling too good. It was Mick's fault for putting too much garam masala in the vindaloo. Phil has an allergy or something. Terrible.'

'And how did that result in the pipe being blocked?'

Doreen rolled her eyes as though talking to a little kid. 'Did you want us to mess up the bathroom as well? Seriously, sometimes you treat me like I'm an immigrant or something. There are laws against discrimination, you know.'

'I'm going out,' Jessica said.

'Where?'

'I have to work.' She didn't, but if she stayed in Doreen's presence another minute she would scream. Or perhaps start throwing things, or both.

Doreen let out a dramatic sigh. 'You can wash up later, then. How am I supposed to do it with a blocked sink?'

There was a pub on the corner that opened at ten o'clock for coffee. Jessica was tempted to wait outside, then burst through the doors and demand an entire bottle of their strongest liquor, but she didn't. Instead, she took a walk around the local park until her anger had dissipated somewhat, then went to Coco Lounge to get a panini for breakfast and read the newspaper.

She began to feel a little better, and started to wonder if her parents' open offer of a place playing lonely, single, on-the-verge-of-thirty daughter on their cruise wouldn't be a better idea than putting up with Doreen over the Christmas season. She had considered speaking to a lawyer about evicting her troublesome housemate, but the last time Doreen had pushed her far enough to threaten it, Doreen had broken down in tears and given a long monologue about how Jessica was her best friend and their time together had made up for a terrible childhood, a dozen or so failed relationships, and blah-de-blah, until Jessica had cracked and agreed she could stay. Still traumatised, Jessica wasn't sure she could handle the same situation again.

The door opened and a young couple came in, bringing with them a gust of cold which rattled Jessica's ankles. She grimaced, wondering why she hadn't sat a little further from the door, then looked up just as the young man took off his jacket and sat down.

When life gives you lemons suck on an orange said the slogan on the back of the sweater he wore. Jessica gave a little smile. Her grandfather's famous catchphrase. It had made him a TV personality during the fifties and sixties, but while his comedy career had graduated to theatre residencies and later cruise ships, careful management of his brand and trademarked catchphrase had made the family rich. Her father, who officially ran Grandpa's estate, but in reality left it to an agency management team who gave him a yearly update, had no problem living off the family fortune. Her mother, herself the daughter of a famous sixties singer, was a perfect match. That Jessica wasn't prepared to sit back and live an easy and carefree life off Grandpa's money had always surprised them.

She turned back to the newspaper, flipping over to the front page. There, in a sidebar she hadn't noticed before was a speculative piece about her grandfather:

Questions remain about the death of classic comic's third wife

Third time lucky? It wasn't for fifties TV comic Ernest Lemond (92), whose third wife Mavis (nee-Brown) (47) died on September 9th after falling from a ladder while replacing tiles on their shared house after a night of rough winds. Brown, a yoga instructor and personal trainer, apparently fell more than twenty feet and was killed instantly. However, questions remain whether the fall was accidental or perhaps something more suspicious. According to sources, Brown had been keen to wrestle back control of Lemond's finances from his only son, Benjamin (58), whom she accused of wasting the family fortune. Lemond, too, was believed to have a strained relationship with his wife, whom he accused of feeding him only liquefied pumpkin soup through a straw for days on end. The case continues. The current whereabouts of Lemond, who is wanted for questioning by local police, are currently unknown.

Jessica shook her head. The police clearly weren't looking too hard. All they had to do was check his Tinder profile or his Instagram, where just yesterday he had posted a picture of a beautiful forested valley which made Jessica dream of getting away. The picture had more than three hundred likes and comments from his fans, none of whom had thought to mention it to the police.

It was tempting to just ignore Dad and let Grandpa get

on with whatever was left of his life, but Jessica had to admit, she was half hoping that the job would come through. It was time for Kirsten to step up anyway; she could handle most of the Christmas season business on her own. Consider it her final exam. Make it to January intact and Jessica would take her on as a partner.

She smiled, realising she was daydreaming, speculating, letting her thoughts throw up random ideas. That was what Doreen did to her: scrambled her mind, left her unsure whether she was coming or going.

Across the room, the young man with the Lemond sweater had suddenly stood up with a scrape of his chair. As his girlfriend gasped with surprise, he dropped to one knee and held up a little box. As the handful of other patrons began to clap, he looked up and said, 'When life gives you lemons, don't suck on an orange. Marry me instead.'

The girl seemed to find this romantic. She burst into a flood of tears, then leapt into his arms, hollering 'Yes, yes, yes!' far louder than was necessary.

With a wry smile, Jessica left a ten pound note on the table for her breakfast and then headed out.

6

OVER THE EDGE

'LOOK, IT WOULD JUST BE FOR A FEW DAYS,' DOREEN said. 'And it's not like you use that sofa much, is it? He wouldn't be any trouble.'

It was rare that Jessica stepped up to battle her housemate, but sometimes a line was drawn that could not be crossed. 'Not a chance,' she said.

Doreen stared at her. 'It's December the first,' she said. 'The first day of Advent?' She gave a sarcastic shake of her head. 'Duh? Weren't you born a Christian?'

'I'm not practicing,' Jessica said.

'But you have a heart, don't you? It's not entirely black and dead. You want to see Mick living on the streets over Christmas, is that it? It's a month, that's all. And it's not like you provide much Christmas cheer, is it? Having Christmas dinner with you I might as well paint the flat black and white and call up the Ghost of Christmas Past. There's more Christmas cheer in *Eastenders*.'

'There's not enough room.'

Doreen planted her hands on her hips and adopted a fighting stance Jessica knew well. It meant she was digging her heels in, taking root like an old tree, and unless Jessica had an axe and was willing to cut her down, she would prove immoveable. Mick—apparently asked to move out of his parents' place because they couldn't keep up with the food bill—was temporarily moving in, whether Jessica liked it or not. And as with so much related to Doreen, temporary could soon mean permanent.

'Oh, I get it. Perfectly obvious now. It's because I told you he liked you. Well, if you want to know, Mick's worth ten of you.'

'He weighs the same as ten of me.'

'Oh, look at you, Little Miss Slimfast. You're a disgraceful excuse for a human being, you know that? I can't believe I put up with you. I should have moved out years ago.'

'The door's right there.'

'So, you're trying to make me homeless for Christmas too? Dickens would be turning in his grave.'

'I'm not—'

Doreen, still standing as though ready to throw out a sharp left hook, suddenly sniffed. A single tear rolled down her cheek. Even though Jessica knew what was coming, she also knew she was about to relent. Mick, all ten thousand tons of him, would be sleeping on her sofa over Christmas. And probably beyond. Most likely until the world eroded around him.

'You have no idea what it's like for people like me,' Doreen sobbed. 'Forever on the fringes of society. Shunned, despised. Laughed at behind my back. You with your mainstream life and your railroad sexuality and your parents who are alive … you have no idea. Is a little sympathy—at Christmas—too much to ask?'

'He moves out January first.'

Doreen stared at her. The tears seemed to dry up like a

puddle beneath the hot desert sun. 'He'll be hungover from New Year,' she said.

'All right, January second.'

Doreen gave a short, terse nod. 'I knew you had a soul,' she said. Jessica wondered if she would go so far as to offer her thanks, but Doreen was done. 'I'll let him know he can come up. He's downstairs with his bags. Cool to have a bit of a moving in bash this evening? Phil's coming round at eight, and might bring a couple of mates. You're working, aren't you?'

Jessica's eyes had glazed over. She picked up her work bag and headed for the door. 'Do whatever you want,' she said. 'I'll be sleeping on the bench across the road in the park.'

'Cool, no worries. I'll tell Phil to give you a nudge on the way home.' Doreen had already turned away, and was holding the TV remote up in one hand, pressing her phone against her ear with the other. Jessica made a hasty exit.

She got outside to find Mick waiting across the street with a suitcase that looked like a child's toy in one massive hand, his phone in the other. An open can of Worthington stood on top of the case. Jessica gave him a wave and he mouthed something that could have been anything. Then she was around the corner and breaking into a run, tears of anger and frustration coursing down her cheeks. She didn't stop until she made it to the Coco Lounge on the corner, its evening disco lights just starting to come on as the last daylight drained out of the day.

Kirsten wasn't due for another half hour, but the last thing on Jessica's mind was the briefing they would usually have before going off to their next evening appointment. She marched straight up to the bar and ordered a double vodka with ice. Downing it in one swallow, then nearly throwing it back up, she ordered a second drink, this time with an orange mixer.

She was about to order a third drink when her phone buzzed. She expected it to be Kirsten, with a usual I'm-on-time-but-I-thought-I'd-better-call-just-in-case-a-volcano-erupts call, but it came from a number she didn't recognise. She went outside to take the call, ducking into an alleyway around the side of the bar.

'Excuse me, is this Miss Jessica Lemond?'

'Speaking. How may I be of help? If you'd wish to make a booking, it's best if you fill out the form on my website—'

'Um, Miss Lemond, this is Snowflake Lodge. You submitted an application for a vacant position?'

'Yes…?'

'This is the general manager of Snowflake Lodge speaking. I'd like to ask you a couple of questions, if I may. We are very interested in your application.'

'Really?'

'Yes. You have all the right qualifications. All I'd like to know about is whether you have the temperament for the position.'

'The temperament?'

'Yes. Can you tell me, with a single sentence answer, why you would be willing to give up whatever it is you're doing and move to a remote Scottish mountain lodge?'

'One sentence?'

'Yes.'

'Well … I live with a maniac who I really don't think wants me dead simply because she enjoys tormenting me so much, and my parents are frighteningly rich, which has made them absent both of emotion and attention for most of my life, but like a good little daughter I still crave their praise and one way to get it is to cross the country in pursuit of a formerly famous grandfather who may or may not have murdered his third wife, while my parents spend an obscene amount of his money on a Christmas cruise of the fjords. Was that one sentence? It might have been two. If so, I apologise.'

There was a pause on the other end of the line, and for a moment Jessica thought she had blown her chance. Then, the man cleared his throat, and said, 'Well, that was quite something. I would have readily accepted 'I enjoy the scenery' or 'I fancy a change', but you certainly made your reasons clear.'

'Sorry about that....'

'In any case, you tick all the boxes for the position. Well, the two boxes that we have, which are a: is a plumber, and b: has applied for the position. So, without further ado … I'd like to offer you the position.'

Jessica jumped about five feet in the air. She was still fist-pumping when a quiet voice from her hand said, 'You can hang up the phone now, if you'd like.'

7

LOOSE ENDS

KIRSTEN WAS SOBBING INTO A TISSUE AND JESSICA FELT like Scrooge all over again. 'It's only for a few weeks,' she said, patting Kirsten on the arm, then handing her another tissue as she paused sobbing just long enough to blow her nose.

'Things were going so well,' Kirsten sniffed. 'Am I not doing a good enough job? I can work harder, you know. Show up earlier—'

'It's not you, it's me,' Jessica said, aware that she was becoming a living caricature of a comic strip character. 'Things have got on top of me of late. I need some time away. It's only a short-term contract. And I know several excellent plumbers who'd be happy to finish off your training.'

'I want to stay with you,' Kirsten blurted, in a rare show of emotion which left Jessica stunned. Usually quiet as the proverbial mouse, it seemed that in her grief Kirsten was belatedly coming alive. 'It wouldn't be the same with someone else. And it's not just that … I was hoping that when my training was finished … you'd take me on. As an assistant.'

Jessica sighed. From one person who couldn't wait to see the back of her, to another developing an obsession. 'Kirsten….'

'I thought we worked so well together. I know it was only supposed to be for a few months, but I thought maybe if I tried really hard, if I studied everything you said….'

Kirsten trailed off, wiping her eyes with a tissue. Jessica stared at her. The truth was that she had planned to take Kirsten on not just as an assistant but a full partner, maybe even when she returned from Snowflake Lodge—*don't say "if"; it's not come to that yet, has it?*—but one reason she wanted to get away was to escape all the drama that was blocking up her forward progress like a knot of toilet tissue in an old u-bend. *And you're going to check up on your former TV star grandfather who also happens to be wanted by the police on suspicion of murder. Escape from drama? Not a chance.*

'Kirsten….'

'Don't say it. Just don't. It's fine. I'm sorry.'

'Kirsten … this is a work contract, so you know, maybe they'll let me bring an assistant….' The words had laid themselves down in a line before she had even really thought about it. She just wanted someone to smile for a change, not cry, not throw things at her, not offer her a fight, and not vomit all over her living room wall.

'Are you sure?'

'I mean, I can't promise anything. I'd have to ask.'

'Oh, Ms Lemond. I don't know what to say.'

Aware people at other tables had begun to stare at them, Jessica wanted to say something more appropriate, but her life felt set in motion like a train on a downward slope without any brakes. 'Just say yes….'

'Yes!' Kirsten wailed, then leaped across the table and pulled Jessica into a hug.

Around them, people at other tables stood up and began to clap.

~

'So Mick can have your bed?'

Jessica shook her head. 'No. Absolutely not. I'm prepared to let Mick stay until he can find somewhere else, but there is literally no way I want him sleeping in my bed. Or anyone else for that matter. If I find anyone's been sleeping in my bed when I get back, I'll hit the roof.'

Doreen smirked. 'And just annoy her upstairs. Oh, Lemons, you have such a way with words. You should have been a poet. So where are you going anyway?'

'I wish I could say Australia, but I can't. Scotland.'

'Ooh, romantic. Who's the lucky man?'

'It's not like that. It's a work thing. I got offered a short-term work contract at a mountain lodge in the Cairngorms. It's a good opportunity to expand my skill base.'

Doreen lifted an eyebrow. 'Wow, you really are taking this turning-thirty thing hard, aren't you? Look, I know you think you're pretty and whatever, and inevitably that's going to start going south as you get older, but do you have to be so desperate?'

'I'm not desperate! I told you, it's a work thing!'

'Full of big muscular guys in skirts and carrying those log things while playing those what-do-you-call-thems made out of sheep's stomachs?'

'Bagpipes?'

'Yeah, those.'

'I'm not sure they're made out of sheep's stomachs, but

whatever. I'm not going to Scotland in order to pick up a guy.'

Although, chance would be a fine thing. She wasn't about to tell Doreen about her grandfather, either. The less ammunition her flat-mate had, the shallower the wounds her next bombardment would leave.

'Well, you have a nice time. We'll be waiting when you get back. I might even go and buy myself a new pair of jeans for your wedding. When do you leave?'

Jessica hadn't thought to ask. The contract started December the eighth, but there was no reason why she had to wait until then. Nothing on her work schedule this week was urgent, so she could put those jobs off until January and perhaps go to Scotland early. Perhaps she could feed Kirsten to the Loch Ness Monster, or even better, herself.

'Tomorrow,' she said.

'Seriously?'

'Yes. Is that a problem?'

Doreen sighed. 'Mick'll be gutted. Arsenal have Bristol Rovers in the Cup on Saturday. He was going to invite you down to Walkabout to watch the game, kind of like a date. Don't tell him I said. Man, if Arsenal win, it'll be something else downtown. Utter carnage.'

Jessica grimaced. 'Tell Mick I'll be sad to miss it. Preferably after I've gone.'

8

WHEELS

Leaving Doreen to her systematic breakdown of everything Jessica had once held dear, she headed off to where it had all begun to go wrong: her parents' house in Clifton. She had planned to ask for any final details or updates, but when she arrived, her parents were uncharacteristically out. Standing on the doorstep, Jessica called her dad.

'Oh, hi, love. What's the matter?'

'I'm standing outside your door, Dad. Where are you? You're not supposed to leave for another week.'

Benjamin chuckled. 'Oh, well, your mother and I decided that we might as well warm up for the cruise with a few days shopping in London. Your mother really couldn't make a decision on which shawl was best, so we thought we'd spend a couple of days on Oxford Street looking for a better one. Oh, and take in a couple of West End shows while we're here. You know, they're showing one at the Redwood Theatre that your grandpa starred in back in the fifties. We did a name-drop and got ourselves box seats. We'll need to pick up some new threads for the show, but won't that be great?'

Jessica balked at the thought of how much of Grandpa's money her parents would be burning through. Rather than feel a sense of resentment that they were living it up on the family fortune while she was slowly being forced out of the little flat on which she was paying a hefty mortgage, she only felt a sense of sadness that they felt no great desire to achieve anything.

'That sounds nice, Dad,' she said. 'Be sure to send me a postcard. Talking of which, have you heard anything else from Grandpa? Anything I ought to be aware of before I drive up there tomorrow?'

'Oh, you're going to drive up, are you? You watch those Scottish roads. Treacherous at the best of times.'

'I'll be careful.'

'If you look in the tin in the kitchen there's some petrol money in there. Your mother was saving grocery change for your Christmas present but since we won't be getting together this year you might as well take it.'

Saving grocery change for your Christmas present. Once the words might have upset her, but Jessica had long ago got used to the otherworldly plane on which her parents appeared to live.

'Thanks, Dad. Where did you leave the key? It's starting to rain.'

'It's in the gnome, of course.'

In the gnome. Of course. Jessica held the phone against her chest as she sighed, then peered into the muddle of potted plants beside the door, wondering where they had hidden the little guy this time. A Christmas present from Jessica to her parents that she had bought with her first pocket money at the age of ten, that they had kept it all these years showed at least how much they loved her, even if hiding the gnome and its prize of the spare key had long been a game/form-of-torture they had insisted on playing on her.

'I'll call you back in a bit, Dad.'

Ricky—the gnome—was nowhere to be seen. Jessica climbed over the smallest row of potted plants at the front, then squeezed past a few larger ones into the very depths of her parents' botanical treasures. Some of the plants left on display on her parents' doorstep were worth more than Jessica's van, something unknown to the petty thieves of Bristol. *Hide your wealth in plain sight* had long been one of her father's favourite catchphrases, even if technically the wealth belonged to Grandpa.

At last she spotted him, poking out of the foliage halfway up the trunk of a rare Bonsai tree, his cheeky grin starting to fade. Jessica pulled him free and turned him over, poking a finger into the little hole between his feet. The key came loose, held inside by a little piece of blu-tac.

She let herself in, pausing to scoop up a pile of letters from her parents' mat. They had a worrying number of advertisements for expensive products and holidays, but buried within them were the usual bank statements and bills. Never one to trust her parents' ability to find their way out of a paper bag, Jessica checked to make sure nothing was immediately due or critical. Safe they weren't going to get Grandpa blacklisted or court-summoned over some unpaid bill, she moved them to a shelf beside the door for her parents to deal with when they returned.

Of more interest were a couple of solicitors' letters, which Jessica debated whether to open or not. In the end, she decided to steam them, so went into the kitchen and set the kettle to boil. While waiting, she went through what was left, finding a couple of flyers addressed to her, and there at the bottom, another postcard from Grandpa.

Greetings, family of mine,

Having a lemon of a time here in sunny Scotland, awaiting the first snow. I feel ten years younger already. Or is that simply the ring of wedding bells on the horizon making me feel that way? Watch this space … and remember, when life gives you lemons, suck on an orange.

Yours faithfully,
Dad / Grandpa

Wedding bells?

He wasn't thinking about it, surely? Not at ninety-two? Jessica had practically given up on the likelihood of ever walking down the aisle and she was yet to touch thirty. With a wry smile she wondered if it would count should Grandpa need a little help. She could only imagine how her parents would be having kittens at the very thought. Grandpa's ten-year marriage to Mavis had driven them bonkers, and for none of the right reasons. A dragon in sheep's clothing, the vile woman had terrorised poor Grandpa, but the only thing that had really concerned Benjamin and Emilia was that Mavis wanted to wrestle back control of Grandpa's fortune. While Jessica had hated Mavis from their very first meeting ('Your nose is a little crooked, isn't it, darling? Perhaps you should stop poking it where it's not wanted.'), she understood why the woman might have wanted to get one over on her jet-setting parents, neither of which would know a real job if it hit them in the face. She found them hard enough to deal with at times herself, and she was their daughter.

Good luck to him, Jessica thought. And if she was there to cheer him on—while standing as close as possible to the booze table—even better. She tucked the postcard into her jacket pocket. She'd tell them when she felt like it.

Aside from the post, her parents' house was in decent order. The gardener, Reg, and the housekeeper, Molly, would be stopping by almost daily, so Jessica had nothing to worry about. As the kettle finished boiling and she picked up the official-looking letters, she almost wondered why she had bothered to come.

The first letter, however, gave her a little tingle of trepidation. A letter from Mavis's solicitor, it informed her parents that Mavis's family intended to fight for compensation in civil court. And the second letter was even worse. It was from a private investigation agency, informing the Lemonds that by the instruction of Mavis's heirs, Grandpa was under suspicion. The police might not be doing much, but if the Lemonds thought they could sit back and relax, they had another think coming.

She left the letters in a tray where she knew her parents would find them, then headed for the door. Kirsten would be waiting for her pick up, and Jessica wanted to be halfway to Scotland by dinner time.

The doorbell rang. Jessica paused, wondering if she should answer it, then figured she might as well. If it was a delivery driver there was no telling when he might catch Molly or Reg at the house, even though the goods were no doubt some unnecessary junk her mother had ordered from the internet.

'Where should I sign?' Jessica said, pulling the door open with one hand, already wielding a pen in the other.

The man on the doorstep glared at her from beneath a wide-brimmed hat. Jessica felt a shiver of fear as those dark, shadowy eyes narrowed. The man, hands deep in the pockets of his trench coat, frowned.

'Emilia Lemond? You're younger than I imagined.

Must be all the expensive facial products.'

Jessica shook her head. 'No, I'm—' She paused. '—Molly. The … um, maid.'

The man lifted a single eyebrow so high it disappeared under the brim of his hat. 'Is that so? Well, in that case, could you pass on a message?'

'Ah, sure. Who should I say called?'

The man withdrew a hand from his pocket which had gold rings across three fingers, none of them his wedding digit. He turned his hand palm up in a sudden smooth motion that reminded Jessica of a magician, and held out a business card.

DICK BURD
Private Investigation Services
Welling Road, Plymouth
No Mystery is Too Deep, No Lie Too Shallow
CALL TODAY FOR A QUOTE

On the back of the card was an atmospheric picture of a man resembling Dick standing on a noir street corner. He certainly played the part, at least.

'Thanks,' Jessica said, trying to sound casual. 'Was there something specific you wanted to talk to them about?'

'It's about the death of Mavis Johns. Let me rephrase that. It's about the *murder* of Mavis Johns.'

Jessica nodded. 'Okay, definitely the murder, not the death? The murder. Is that right?'

'Golden,' Dick said. 'You could have a career in the industry yourself if you were prepared to consider giving up folding bed sheets. In fact I wouldn't be adverse to being part of a husband-and-wife team.'

Delivered in the same deadpan caricature, it took

Jessica a minute to pick up on the rather roundabout proposition. Against her better judgment, she found herself blushing.

'Um, well, I appreciate the offer, but I'm afraid I'm already … betrothed.'

The archaic word came out before she could think of something more appropriate, and Jessica found herself sweating as well as blushing.

'No betrothal can pass unchallenged,' Dick said, his face and voice deadpan. Jessica began to wonder if some hidden camera crew were about to jump out of her parents' expensive porch flora. Perhaps Doreen had set it up because Jessica had refused to go rioting with Mick on a first date.

'Well, I'd better get back to work,' Jessica said, forcing an awkward chuckle. 'I'll be sure to pass on your card and your message. No doubt M—my *employers* … will get back to you as soon as is convenient.'

With a satisfied nod, Dick Burd wished her good day with a tip of his hat, then retreated to the street. However, there he stayed, talking into a mobile phone while Jessica peeked out of the living room curtains.

She couldn't just leave because her ruse would be blown, but Kirsten was waiting and Jessica was keen to get out of her parents' house. There was no way out through the garden, because it was backed by high walls which bordered other gardens, and the type of people who lived alongside her parents didn't tolerate people garden-hopping. She would get electrocuted, snared, or have her foot chewed off by a guard dog. She shook her head. The garden was a no go.

Then she remembered her father's basement garage. It led down a slope under the house, its door shared with the neighbours' place, which might have confused Dick Burd.

Extremely secure from the outside to protect her father's man-toys, from the inside it was easily accessed through a door in the kitchen. A key inside a teapot shaped like a London bus on the kitchen window ledge opened the door at the bottom of a set of stairs, and Jessica let herself in. Her parents had taken the Benz, she saw, perhaps to leave it in an expensive long-stay car park somewhere in Dover, where they were due to board the cruise ship. The BMW was still there, but Jessica gave it only a passing glance, her gaze fixing on her father's newest toy, sitting in the third bay, the one usually left empty for guests.

A motorcycle and sidecar. Jessica stared. To the best of her knowledge, her father didn't even have a license, but knowing him, he had probably bought one online or somewhere else which only rich people could use to get whatever they wanted with the least amount of effort.

She went closer, walking around it. She had seen a few on the road, but never up close. However, back during her late teens, during a brief period of rebellion, she had dated a guy who was into motorbikes, and he had pushed her into taking a test so that they could go riding together. Just like her unwanted nickname, that relationship had turned sour, but it had left Jessica with something she hadn't even remembered until now.

She slipped her hand into her bag, pulling out her purse. Her drivers' license was in there, the check in the category box for motorcycles plain to see. It had been nearly ten years, but it hadn't been that hard … a couple of turns up and down a quiet street wouldn't hurt, and if she wore one of her father's helmets she could hide her identity from Dick Burd, if he was still outside. A little spin around town, give him time to get bored and go home … no problem.

She took a helmet down off a shelf and tried it on. It fit

perfectly and smelled brand new: it was probably one Benjamin had bought for her mother but she was yet to use. Jessica climbed onto the bike's seat and rested her hands on the throttle. It felt remarkably comfortable, and the sidecar gave it a stability that a regular motorbike didn't have. It would be no more difficult than driving her van, just a little windier and a whole lot cooler.

As she pretended to twist the throttle, a sudden thought struck her.

No.

Scotland was a long, long way.

I can't really be thinking about this, can I?

The bike was a monster, a classic Matchless Tomahawk, built for touring. The sidecar had plenty of room for luggage as well as a passenger. And her tools wouldn't take up much space….

With the helmet on, she barely heard the roar of the engine as she turned the key, but beneath her the cold lump of metal had become a humming, powerful beast. The bike she had taken her test on had been a mere cow compared to this dragon, but as she turned the throttle and felt the engine's power, she certainly saw the appeal. And it would be a far more interesting ride to Scotland than her old van would have been.

'Merry Christmas, Dad and Mum,' she whispered. 'Thanks for the present.'

With a grin, she pressed the door control her father had conveniently taped to the bike's petrol tank, waiting as the huge automatic doors rose up into the ceiling. A minute later she was roaring past a bemused Dick Burd, who was still standing on the pavement outside her parents' house with his phone pressed to his ear.

In the wing mirror, she watched with amusement as his hat flew off his head and landed in the middle of the road.

9

ROAD HOGS

Kᴛʀsᴛᴇɴ's ᴍᴏᴜᴛʜ ᴄʀɪɴᴋʟᴇᴅ ɪɴᴛᴏ ᴀ ᴘᴏʟɪᴛᴇ ɢʀɪᴍᴀᴄᴇ. She rubbed at the side of her eye as though anticipating a tear, and shook her head, a spare helmet Jessica had found in the sidecar held awkwardly in front of her like something alien

'I'm afraid I don't think I can do this.'

'Don't worry. The sidecar's even got a fold-out roof if it starts to rain. It's no different than a car. Not really.'

'But it's so flimsy. What if a lorry overturns in front of us? It'll squash us flat.'

'I don't think we'd fair much better in the van,' Jessica said. 'Look, these are our wheels. I've kind of borrowed them now and can't take them back.' It was true; the front door key was still on her parents' kitchen table and, following a spin on the M32 to see what the bike could do, the door control taped to the petrol tank had flown off and landed in the central reservation somewhere. She had no way back into her parents' house except to show up and hope Reg or Molly were there. And without being able to get back in, she had no way to check their schedules.

'I hope you're insured.'

'No problem. Dad always puts me on his friends and family plan.'

'And you've ridden before, I gather?'

'Loads of times.' *Not in ten years,* she neglected to say. *And then on nothing remotely as powerful as this behemoth.*

'Well, I suppose if we have no other choice....'

After a little more goading, Kirsten got into the sidecar and they set off. It felt incredible to be out on the open road, the wind billowing around her, and with her helmet on she could barely hear the engine, let alone Kirsten's screams. For the first time in years she felt free.

Just after turning onto the M5 to head north, they saw the first roadworks sign. Ten minutes later they were in standstill traffic. Jessica turned to the sidecar to make some witty comment about the trials of the road, but much to her frustration, Kirsten, leaning on an inflatable pillow, was fast asleep.

'Oh, I suppose anything, really,' Kirsten said, lifting her head from the book just long enough to look at Jessica across the table, whose latest attempt to start a decent conversation looked like it was falling just as flat as the others. 'Whatever I can find.'

'So, like horror, or mystery? Romance?'

Kirsten shrugged. 'Whatever I have on hand.'

She looked ready to bury her head back into her book, judging by the atmospheric cover a mystery by a writer Jessica had never heard of called Jack Benton. Jessica, who couldn't bear the thought of eating in silence while Kirsten read, leaned sideways, trying to get a look at the blurb on the back cover. Something about a man who had gone missing.

'Do you always read at dinner time?'

Kirsten closed the book and shrugged. 'No, not always. Mostly just when I'm … nervous.'

Jessica smiled. 'Are you nervous now? We work together, remember?'

Kirsten gave an awkward shrug, and Jessica wondered if this was how her parents had felt on the few occasions they had taken her out to restaurants as a teenager. 'But we've never really hung out, have we? And, you know, you're the boss.'

'But I'm not like a dragon boss or anything, am I?'

It was meant as a joke, but Kirsten just gave a polite smile. 'You treat me fairly,' she said. 'I couldn't ask for more.'

The waiter arrived with their food. Kirsten closed the book but left it on the tabletop, as though threatening that it could be picked up and resumed at any time. She waited politely for Jessica to pick up her knife and fork, then picked up her own and sat waiting for Jessica to begin eating. As Jessica cut into her first chip, then waited for Kirsten to make a tentative poke at one of her own, Jessica felt something inside her snap. She put her knife and fork down with a sharp crack, making Kirsten flinch.

'Look,' she said, 'We're in a Holiday Inn in the middle of the Midlands somewhere. We're not due to arrive at Snowflake Lodge for another week, so if we end up getting drunk and being too hungover to do anything other than fester in our rooms all tomorrow, then that's fine, right?'

Kirsten looked like her puppy had just died. She gave a brief, bullied nod.

'Do you know what I did today?'

Kirsten shook her head this time. 'You ordered battered haddock and chips?'

'No, Kirsten, not that,' Jessica said, feeling a strange kind of euphoria coming over her. 'Something much more important. I escaped from my basket case of a lodger. Do you know what tonight is?'

'Tuesday?'

'It's my first night of freedom. So what if she's wrecking my flat with her feral mates? I don't care. I'm on the road, with my, um, employee—'

'Technically government-appointed trainee—'

'—and friend. Do you really think I want to let tonight pass me by?'

'Well, it hasn't yet. It's only eight o'clock.'

'We have to celebrate, Kirsten.' Jessica lifted a hand in the air and clicked her finger for the waiter, then immediately realised it was something her parents might have done and began to profusely apologise as he came over, a bemused look on his face. She ordered a bottle of Lambrusco with two glasses —because her parents would have ordered champagne—plus a beer for the waiter to drink after his shift. The waiter filled their glasses and Jessica handed one to Kirsten.

'She might have taken my flat, but she'll never take my freedom!'

'Well, that's something, isn't it?' Kirsten said.

They drank, Jessica a little more enthusiastically than Kirsten, but at least something mildly alcoholic passed her young protégé's lips. She might be able to force a party yet.

With their hotel at the end of a motorway service area somewhere past Wolverhampton, they were literally in the middle of nowhere. The hotel had one onsite bar, which Jessica insisted they visit after dinner. The only other customers were an elderly couple, but Jessica had soon goaded them into a karaoke contest using a dusty setup dragged out from under a sheet in a corner. Her ridiculous crooning was put to shame by their note perfect renditions of various classic continental hits, while even Kirsten, eventually forced to take on a bland Westlife ballad, managed to outdo her. The success was in the pudding, however, with Jessica stumbling back to her room with a sense of achievement unlike any other: she had managed to drink Doreen off her mind.

Kirsten helped her to take off her shoes, then wished her good night. Jessica slumped down on her bed and reached for her phone on the bedside table where she had left it, the colours and numbers blurring as she used her thumb print to unlock the home screen.

She had only wanted to know what time it was—a pathetically unadventurous 11.15 p.m.—but the messages-received icon was lit up. Too drunk to resist what she was afraid of seeing, she immediately winced as Doreen's name appeared on the screen.

The toilet cistern's popped off the wall. I think a couple of screws were loose. When Mick sat down it just popped right off. The poor chap nearly face-planted on the back of the door. Seriously, you need to get this fixed. I believe that it's my right to hold back my rent until you get someone in.

Jessica groaned. She opened the message box to write some sarcastic or borderline aggressive reply, but her creative well was dry. *Okay*, she typed, then closed her phone, closed her eyes, and went to sleep.

10

ROAD TROUBLES

'Are you sure you're okay to drive?' Kirsten said, peering over a plate of salad vegetables. 'I mean, you don't look too well this morning. How much did you drink?'

'Not enough,' Jessica said. 'Doreen still managed to get me.'

'Oh? What's happened?'

Kirsten nodded while Jessica explained. When she was done, Kirsten said, 'I suppose you could call someone out to take a look. It shouldn't be hard to fix as long as the plumbing is intact.'

'That's beside the point,' Jessica said. 'It wasn't broken yesterday morning when I left. I should have her evicted, but I need the money.'

'That's too bad,' Kirsten said, then glanced over her shoulder, through the window at the car park, where the Tomahawk was parked against the curb. 'Forgive me if I'm speaking out of place, but aren't your parents quite well off?'

Jessica laughed. 'Well off is an understatement. My father is the heir to one of the greatest fortunes in show

58

business. And all because my grandfather was clever enough to trademark several of his most famous catchphrases.'

'So couldn't they lend you any money?'

Jessica sighed. 'As soon as I was old enough to understand the situation, I wanted no part of it. Sure, it would be nice to be rich and not have to work, but what's the point? Your whole life has no meaning.'

Kirsten just gave half a shrug as she chewed on a raw carrot. 'But it would make things easier.'

'I stole—I mean, borrowed—that bike. I think they've given me enough for one trip.'

'So what's the plan for today?'

'We head on up to Scotland. It might take us a day or two to find the place, because according to the brochure it's in an internet black spot. Then we'll have a few days to settle in before we get to work. You know, have a look at the place, check out the other staff and guests, maybe take a few walks or hit up one of the local towns.'

'Sounds interesting. Like a proper girly trip.'

The way Kirsten said it sounded awkward, as though it was a phrase she had read in a magazine and memorised for future use. Jessica gave her a humouring smile.

'Yeah, that's right.'

They packed up and headed out. As Jessica climbed back on to the Tomahawk, she discovered something she hadn't previously known about riding motorcycles: it took a while for your bum to adjust to the new angles. Sure, the seat felt nice and soft but her inner thighs felt like she had been through a rigorous yoga session and her lower back had a bruise-like pain which flared whenever they went over a bump. Wincing with each jolt in the road, she steered them back onto the motorway.

At a service area an hour north, a couple of

paracetamol helped her back as well as her head. Kirsten wandered off to the loo, so Jessica headed into a newsagent to browse the magazine rack. Trying to keep her mind off work, she ignored the working magazines section which she usually enjoyed, instead trying to find an interest in the countryside and nature section. She had just picked up a copy of *Horse & Hound* when a hat emerging from a car outside the window caught her eye.

'You've got to be having a laugh....'

Dirk Burd, looking suspiciously like he was searching for someone, walked across the plaza from the car park, hands stuffed into the pockets of his trench coat, eyes darting about. He had parked almost directly behind their motorcycle, as though he had trailed them all the way from Bristol.

He entered through a main door leading to an open promenade between the shops, passing almost directly in front of her. She ducked down, just as Kirsten appeared through the door.

'Miss Lemond—I mean, um, Jessica—what are you doing?' Kirsten said, in a voice which seemed traitorously loud, considering the circumstances. Jessica flapped a hand, indicating to Kirsten to crouch down alongside.

'Did you see the man in the hat?'

'The man in the yellow hat?' Kirsten said in another bad attempt at a joke as she glanced at a rack of children's DVDs. 'Perhaps he was monkeying about?'

Jessica winced. 'No, the hat was more of a dark grey-brown. He went into the cafeteria.'

'Was he a bit of alright?'

Jessica felt a growing urge to scream. The next time they had a moment alone, she needed to explain to Kirsten what decade they currently resided in.

'No, far from it,' she said. 'I think he's following me.'

She explained about the visit from Dick Burd to her parents' house. 'I thought I gave him the slip, but he must have somehow figured out where we were going.'

'It's a bit of a coincidence, isn't it? Perhaps he's a travelling salesman by day and only a private investigator by night.'

'Maybe, but I don't know.'

'It's all a little fishy, isn't it?' Kirsten said, then immediately burst into raucous laughter which sounded even worse when she abruptly cut it off.

'Let's get out of here,' Jessica said.

They headed for the exit. They had just climbed back on to the bike when a sudden shout came from across the plaza.

'Oh dear,' Kirsten said, as Dick Burd appeared, holding something up in his hands. Jessica, who managed to drop the key on the ground, could only look up helplessly as Dick Burd hurried across the outside courtyard towards them. Then, just as she was wondering whether to play innocent or accuse him of stalking, he hailed an old lady standing at the car beside his own.

'Excuse me, madam, but you dropped your car key,' he said, holding up the set of keys and giving them an emphatic little jingle.

'Oh, deary me,' the old lady said. 'What a kind young man you are. I was looking everywhere for those. I thought we might have been marooned here all afternoon.'

As she reached up and gave Dick Burd's cheek an affectionate pinch and tug, Jessica retrieved the bike's key and started the engine. As she pulled away, it was telling that Dick Burd didn't look in their direction. Perhaps that was just a ploy, though. He was a wily character after all.

A couple of hours later, as they pulled into another service area in order to give Jessica's aching rear end a break, Kirsten climbed out of the sidecar and said, 'Are you sure you weren't driving just a little fast back there?'

Jessica grimaced. She had definitely worked the throttle, that was for sure. Both her aching bum and the fear that Dick Burd might be following them had urged her to go a little quicker than she might have liked.

'I mean, it might have just been the sun's reflection, but I was sure a couple of speed cameras flashed.'

Jessica shrugged. 'I wasn't going that fast.' *But if I was, Dad will have to foot the bill. Maybe he'll just report the bike as stolen, since he was in London at the time, and maybe I'll get arrested and lose my business and end up in the slammer and become a lifelong criminal and Doreen will never move out of my flat—*

'Probably just a reflection,' Kirsten said. 'Is it teatime yet? Shall we get some grubber?'

'Some … oh, food.'

It was just after three o'clock. They were an hour past Edinburgh and by Jessica's reckoning should be at Snowflake Lodge by six. According to the map she had gotten from the internet, they had another couple of hours on decent roads, then it was into the hills. With a machine like the Tomahawk, it ought to be exhilarating.

They had just collected their food and sat down in the window of a Tasty Chef, when a familiar figure walked past on the concourse outside. With a hat pulled down over his eyes Jessica couldn't see his face, but the trench coat and the way he walked were a dead giveaway.

'He's following me,' she said.

'Oh, does that mean we're on the run?' Kirsten said with a giggle.

'Are you enjoying this?'

'Well, it is quite exciting, isn't it? I don't think I've ever been a fugitive before.'

'We're not fugitives. He's a private investigator. He's not even a proper policeman.'

'But he's probably busted loads of crims.'

Jessica sighed. 'I doubt he's busted any *crims*,' she said. 'Look. I've had enough of this. I'm going to confront him and tell him to stop following us.'

Before Kirsten could say anything, Jessica stood up and marched out of the restaurant, feeling a sense of power she wished she could have drummed up in the battle against Doreen. Perhaps it was being on the road, or having the Tomahawk instead of her old transit van, or that she was back in her role as Kirsten's boss. Whatever it was, she was ready to open up a massive can of whoop-ass as she pushed through the door onto the concourse, her fists already bunched, her jaw set, eyes glaring like lasers—

'Come on, dear, hold on to my arm.'

Jessica stopped. Just a couple of steps in front of her, Dick Burd was helping an old lady with a walker to cross the concourse from the restaurant to a bookshop on the other side. Jessica glowered at the back of his hat, wanting it to explode, but her anger felt doused by a large bucket of icy water.

'Oh, what a kind young man you are,' said the old lady. 'In my day, everyone was brought up right, but these days they're all hooligans. Your mother did a good job with you, young man. If I could give you a kiss, I would.'

'That's quite all right,' Dick Burd said, not a hint of disrespect or repulsion in his voice. In fact, had he not been a private investigator, he would have looked like a perfect care worker. 'We're nearly there. With everyone rushing about, you have to be so careful.'

'You're such a kind young man. I want to buy a

souvenir for my grandson. Do you have time to spare a minute?'

'Of course I do. What does he like?'

'He's into his trains, is my little Jimmy.'

'Well, I see they sell a few model railways, so why don't we call an assistant and ask what's popular?'

'Oh, what a thoughtful young man you are. Are you married? I have a niece who's still single. She's getting a little long in the tooth, but she still brushes up all right when she does her make-up.'

'No, I'm still single,' Dick Burd said.

'Well, some lucky lady is missing out,' the old lady said. 'If I were sixty-five years younger….'

Jessica had heard enough. She ran back into the restaurant to where Kirsten was just finishing off her salad.

'We have to go. He's buying train sets. Let's move.'

'Don't you want to finish your lunch?'

Jessica looked at her untouched heap of greasy eggs and bacon and shrugged. 'I suppose it's time I started eating a little healthier,' she said. 'I'll grab a chocolate bar on the way out.'

'I noticed they were stocking a new brand of soy bars in the newsagent,' Kirsten said. 'They're a little dry unless you drink something with them, but you soon adjust to the taste. And it is for the environment, after all.'

Jessica figured she would mull over how a soy bar would help the environment once she was back in the Tomahawk's saddle.

'Quick,' she said. 'While he's distracted.'

They headed back out to the motorcycle and hit the road. After an hour of cruising only a little above the speed limit in order to appease Kirsten, Jessica began to relax. Surely it was just a coincidence? Perhaps Dick Burd had family who lived up in Scotland. Christmas was coming, after all, and she imagined private investigators worked on a pretty flexible schedule.

Just in case, however, she decided to pull off the motorway a couple of exits early. With the sun just setting, the light was poor on the motorway anyway, so she put the headlights on full beam and cruised through some quiet villages as the hills began to steepen, the road to narrow and meander more. As the last twilight illuminated the looming peaks of distant mountains, Jessica wondered whether it might have been better to stop somewhere for the night and experience the Scottish scenery in the morning. It was getting colder, and in the sidecar beside her Kirsten had pulled down the rain cover and was dozing with her head on the inflatable pillow. Suddenly, with the headlight illuminating nothing but roads and stone walls, Jessica began to feel lonely.

At six o'clock she stopped in a tiny village which was little more than a couple of houses and a phone box. Underneath a street light she pulled out her phone, found she had no reception, so instead unfolded the printout of the map she had got from the internet.

Where it had seemed so clear at the time of printing, now it was a featureless spider web of unlabeled lines with the lodge in the middle. Jessica couldn't even be sure if they had made it on to the map or not.

With the bike idling, Kirsten woke up and looked around them, rubbing sleep out of her eyes.

'Oh, is this it? I was expecting something a little more grandiose, but it has a certain charm.'

'This is definitely not it,' Jessica said, looking around at the cluster of stone-walled houses. 'I'm not sure where we are, but this is definitely not Snowflake Lodge.'

'Just have a look inside the phone box,' Kirsten said. 'It'll have a sign somewhere to say which locality it is.'

At such a practical suggestion, Jessica wondered if she was losing her mind. She nodded thanks, then wandered into the phone box to check it out.

Locfaer.

She wasn't sure if that was a village or a county, but there was definitely a Locfaer labeled on her map. She looked at the two intersecting roads that converged just past the phone box and made an educated guess at which one led to the lodge, located in the map's centre.

'Got it,' she said. 'Let's go. Not far now.'

But it was far. An hour later, with the last of the day long behind them, and a freezing Scottish wind whistling down the country lanes, they pulled up at another village that looked remarkably like the one they had just passed.

'Are we there yet?' Kirsten said. 'It's getting a little chilly, isn't it? Do you want me to break out the coffee?'

Wondering whether her long-dead grandma had somehow possessed Kirsten's body, Jessica shook her head. 'Let's keep it for a celebration when we finally arrive. Wait here a minute. I'll go and check in that phone box.'

'I'm pretty sure this is—'

Jessica opened the phone box door and groaned.

'—the same place we were in before.'

Locfaer.

'I think we should have taken the other fork,' Jessica said.

'Oh dear. Are you sure you wouldn't like me to get out the coffee? Then we can put our thinking hats on and solve this mystery.'

Jessica closed her eyes for a long moment, taking a couple of deep breaths. *I survived Doreen. I can survive this. Actually, I didn't really survive Doreen. I fled like a coward in a lion's den. Life sucks.*

'We'll just take the other fork,' Jessica said. 'It was a

small mistake. We got to see a little of the countryside, though didn't we?'

'Oh yes,' Kirsten said, with more enthusiasm than was necessary, considering that all they had seen for the last hour was a circle of road twenty feet in front of them.

They got back onto the bike and headed off. They had only gone a couple of miles when something began to flash on the dashboard. Jessica looked down, a feeling of terrible dread coming over her.

They were running out of petrol.

The last petrol station they had seen had been on the motorway. The light was just a warning, though; there would be a little left in the tank. And they weren't far, surely? Snowflake Lodge had to be just around the corner.

Half an hour of worried riding later, however, the engine wheezed and died. With no power, they freewheeled to the bottom of the hill and came to a stop on a little stone bridge crossing a trickling stream. No road signs, no buildings, and over the stone walls bordering the road there wasn't even proper pasture land to suggest they were near a settlement, just lumpy, rocky moor.

'I think we have a problem,' Jessica said.

'Have we run out of petrol? Oh dear.'

'That just about sums it up,' Jessica said.

'You'd better turn off the lights, otherwise we'll use up the battery too,' Kirsten said. 'Never mind. I packed a torch, and we have the coffee. If we snuggle up next to each other in the sidecar we can probably keep warm.'

Jessica let out a long sigh. She killed the lights, waited for her eyes to adjust, and then looked around. The sky was thankfully clear, and a half moon illuminated a desolate moorland valley stretching away in one direction, rising into mountains in the other, with the stream cutting down the middle. It would have been beautiful if they weren't faced with a cold night huddling in the sidecar. She still had no phone reception, and they hadn't seen a single other vehicle since leaving the motorway. They were well and truly lost.

'It'll be like camping,' Kirsten said, sounding far more excited than Jessica felt. 'I think I have some marshmallows in my bag. And my phone's fully charged. I downloaded a few Christmas movies before we set off. It'll be like a girls' night in.'

Jessica couldn't help but smile. Despite the dread she felt, Kirsten's excitement was catching.

'I wonder what marshmallows taste like dipped in coffee,' she said.

'I have a pack of coffee-flavoured,' Kirsten said with a shy smile, as though they were a pet love. 'And strawberry. Tesco had a two-for-one on.'

'Well, at least we won't starve,' Jessica said, at almost the exact moment a sudden snort came out of the darkness from the other side of the stone wall where they had stopped.

For a terrifying moment the two looked at each other, neither daring to breathe. 'Something else won't either,' Kirsten said in a hollow voice.

A second snort—closer than the first—threw Jessica into action. 'Quick, into the sidecar,' she said, pushing Kirsten ahead of her.

The sidecar only had one seat, but by squeezing in sideways they could both just about fit inside. Getting as comfortable as she could, Jessica pulled the cover over the top of them.

'What do you think it is?' Kirsten said. 'Don't they have bears in Scotland?'

'I don't think so, but they definitely have mountain lions.'

'What about wolves?'

'Wolves howl, don't they? It didn't sound like a wolf.'

'Perhaps it was a cow.'

'We're in the middle of nowhere. It's far more likely from some illegal zoo hidden out here on the moor.'

'Like a grizzly bear?'

'Who knows?'

'It sounded like a walrus. I saw one once in a zoo.'

Despite expecting to be eaten alive within the next few minutes, Jessica found this incredibly funny. She coughed a wild laugh just as something pressed against the rain cover and snorted, covering the plastic with steam.

Both girls screamed.

The creature didn't seem to care, whatever it was. It nosed at the cover as though trying to open it.

'Don't eat us!' Kirsten shouted. 'We're too young to die!'

'Don't worry,' came a man's voice from behind the motorbike. 'She won't eat you. She just wants to be your friend.'

11

JAMES

'It's a man,' Kirsten said, rather stating the obvious. 'Have you ever seen *Wrong Turn*? I think we made one.'

'Let's not panic,' Jessica whispered. Then, raising her voice, she said, 'What do you want? You can take the bike, but leave us alone.'

The man, sounding right outside, laughed. 'I appreciate your offer on such a fine vehicle, but it's out of petrol by the look of things, and within an hour or so you'll be out of heat unless you're all wrapped up warm.'

'Does this cover have a lock?' Kirsten asked.

'It's light Perspex,' Jessica said. 'You could cut it open with a butter knife.'

'Better just to use the zip, rather than damage it,' the man said, one hand tapping on the plastic, making the two women jump. 'Don't worry, neither me nor the reindeer bite.'

'Reindeer?'

'Come on out and meet Belinda. Then we'll get you somewhere warm where you can rest overnight.'

'We will not go easily to your love dungeon,' Kirsten said, pulling a wrench out of Jessica's tool bag. 'You'll have to beat us into submission.'

'My what? Have you been breathing too many petrol fumes?'

Jessica took the wrench out of Kirsten's hands and put it back into the bag. 'Let me deal with this,' she said, unzipping the cover and folding it back.

She stood up, looking around her. The man was standing with a lantern in one hand on the other side of the bike. In the other he was holding the bridle of an enormous reindeer. As Jessica stared, the reindeer snorted and stamped its hooves with impatience. Something silvery dripped off its back, and to Jessica's surprise she realised it was melting snow.

'Oh, um, hello,' she said.

The man turned. He was perhaps a little older than her, mid-thirties. His face a little stubby, hair a little rugged. He wore a woolly hat and a thick sweater that looked like it had been made from the wool of three or four sheep.

'Hi. We heard you come down the valley earlier. I'm not sure where you're heading, but you're off most of the touring routes. Far too windy for most bikers out here. You ran out of petrol?'

Jessica blushed. *Why am I blushing?* 'Yeah, looks like it.'

'Is this your bike?'

'Ah … kind of.'

'Kind of?'

'It's my dad's.'

The man smiled. 'Oh. Well, he has good taste. Must have cost a few quid.'

'Yeah, I think so.' She wondered why she felt like she was digging herself a hole. Trying to correct herself, she said, 'I'm Jessica and this is my, um, friend, Kirsten.'

'Government-appointed trainee,' Kirsten said, standing up. 'This is the first time we've done anything girly together.'

Jessica grimaced. 'We're on our way to Snowflake Lodge.'

'Oh, really? We'll you're a little ways off. You missed a turn back along, but it's not far. Half an hour on these roads. About the same by sled.'

'Sled?'

The man smiled again. He had a nice smile, Jessica thought, even if it felt a little patronising. 'Yeah, once the snow sets in, it's the best way to get around. Belinda here needs the exercise too.'

'Are you like, Father Christmas?' Kirsten blurted.

'Do I look that old?'

'About thirty-five.'

The man laughed. 'I'm thirty-four. But I'll give you a year for the poor lighting. My name's James. James Wilcox. And down there by the train line, that's my cousin Henry.'

'Henry?'

James cupped his hands and hollered, 'Henry! Up here! I've got her!'

A light appeared further down the valley, quickly moving upslope. A figured appeared out of the dark and another man, a couple of years older but just as powerfully built and—reluctantly, Jessica had to admit—handsome, came up to meet them. For some reason, the first thing she noticed was the ring on his finger.

Kirsten, rather shockingly, had noticed it too. 'Oh, you're married?' she said. 'I suppose this can't be like the movies, then. Two guys, two gals?' She pronounced it with a long, drawling "a" as though it were something she had copied from a movie. Jessica closed her eyes, wishing she had some duct tape to put over Kirsten's mouth. 'Not that it matters, because I have a boyfriend.'

Jessica's eyes snapped open. 'Since when?

'Last week. Billy from the pub asked me out on a date. We haven't been on it yet, but we will.'

'You never told me.'

'Of course not. You're my boss.'

James and Henry were both chuckling. Jessica felt like a seventeen-year-old away from home for the first time.

'Do you think you could point us in the direction of the nearest petrol station?' she asked.

James laughed. 'Thirty miles back the way you came. If you start walking you'll be there by morning, if the bears don't get you first.'

'Bears? There are bears?' Kirsten said.

'And wolves. But no walruses. You're safe there.'

Jessica's cheeks burned as the two men shared an amused glance. She decided she didn't like either of them much at all.

'We'll wait until morning,' she said. 'We'll be fine here in the sidecar. It was nice to meet you both, but we'll let you get on your way.'

James's smile dropped, replaced by an expression of seriousness Jessica had not seen before. 'I'm afraid we can't allow that,' he said. 'It's December. It's not proper cold yet but in three or four hours it'll start to kick in. It could easily go ten below tonight, and it's snowing further up the valley. It's a good thing she got over the fence or we might never have found you.'

'Well, we appreciate the help,' Jessica said.

'You said you were heading for Snowflake Lodge?'

'Yes.'

James nodded. 'We're on foot, and it'll get a little icy to

go up there tonight, but there's plenty of room at my place. It's about a twenty-minute-walk along the train line.'

He had mentioned the train line before, but Jessica hadn't seen anything. 'Where?'

James pointed over his shoulder. 'It's about a hundred yards in front of you,' he said. 'It goes from Inverness out to Hollydell, where Henry lives. It's another ten miles further east.'

'Hollydell?'

Henry smiled. 'It's a Christmas village. You should visit while you're up here, if you have a chance. Say, are you girls from down south?'

'Bristol,' Jessica said.

'You should meet my wife, Maggie. She's a southern girl too. She's visiting her family at the moment, but she'll be back around Christmas. How long are you up here on holiday?'

'Oh, we're not on holiday,' Jessica said, immediately wishing she'd gone with Henry's assumption.

'No?'

'She's the new plumber,' Kirsten said proudly. 'And I'm her assistant.'

The men shared another glance. 'Is that so? Working women?'

'But we're not lesbians,' Kirsten said.

Jessica put her head in her hands and moaned as the two men laughed. 'I prefer you when you're reading your books, Kirsten,' she said.

James clapped his hands together. 'Come on, let's get out of this cold, just in case there are any bears. Bring whatever you need. We'll hunt out a tank of petrol from the shed and one of us'll come out for the bike in a bit.'

A few minutes later, they were following James and Henry's bobbing lanterns, the huge reindeer trotting obediently along beside them. They crossed a train line that had been entirely hidden in the dark, then James turned up a narrow track leading between two stone walls. The train line was on one side, the hill rising off into darkness on the other. As the trail began to rise, moving away from the train line and angling uphill, they passed patches of wet snow on the ground.

'We're a week or so off the first big dumps,' James said. 'Once it comes it's here until March, though. It's snowshoes and sleds all round.'

'Isn't that a bit inconvenient?'

James smiled. 'Not when you've got a tummy full of hot chocolate, there are lights hanging in the trees, and a fire burning in the grate. You get used to it. Ah, here we are.'

The path angled around a corner to reveal a cluster of farm buildings set around a small but quaint farmhouse. Set into a hollow in the hill, its lights had been entirely invisible from the road, which Jessica guessed was somewhere to the east behind them. Outside lights illuminated a cobblestone courtyard, in the centre of which was a large pine tree.

'If you have time in the morning, I'd love a little help decorating my tree,' James said.

They took Belinda to a barn, in which several other reindeer sat on the ground, apparently asleep. A couple stood up at Belinda's arrival, wandering over to the gate to see what was going on.

'Aren't they huge?' Kirsten said.

'They need to be if they're going to pull Father Christmas's sleigh,' James said. 'It's pretty full, you know. Did you know that he needs to visit eight hundred and twenty-two houses per second in order to visit every house on Christmas Eve?'

'I didn't know that,' Kirsten said. 'Does that take into account the number of children per house, or the respective religions of their parents?'

James looked awkward. 'I suppose it depends on which book of interesting facts you read.'

Henry offered to go and get the bike, while James let them inside. The house was a traditional cottage, all stone walls and lamp-lit nooks and comfortable armchairs, with a log fire in the living room. James took them in and sat them down, then returned a few minutes later with a tray of hot chocolate and marshmallows.

'This will fill you up,' he said. 'We might as well get into the spirit of things with Christmas just around the corner. Just so you don't get too much of a sugar high, I'm reheating some stew from dinner. Give me a few minutes.'

Jessica was surprised to see it was nearly nine o'clock. Kirsten, humming to herself, set about making some kind of marshmallow tower on top of her hot chocolate. Jessica looked around the room, taking in all the mementoes and family photographs. Most of them showed an elderly couple, but in older photographs she recognised a young boy as James, standing beside a girl who was a little older.

'My family,' he said, coming back in with a tray laden with bowls of stew and large crusty bread rolls. 'My parents have sadly passed. My sister, Lillian, lives down in London. She's got some posh city job. It was left to me to take over our parents' farm.'

'You live here alone?'

He smiled. 'Just me and my cat, Molly,' he said, just as Kirsten sneezed.

'Are you all right?'

Kirsten flapped a hand. 'Oh dear. I have some tablets in my bag, don't worry. Ah, but I left them with the bike.'

'Henry will be here in a minute. Sit on that chair over there. Molly doesn't like that one.'

Jessica grimaced as Kirsten sneezed again.

'Oh, bless me.'

Just at that moment, the front door opened and Henry came in, a swirl of wind bringing a flurry of snow with him. He shut the door, pulled off his coat, and gave them a smile.

'All good,' he said. 'I've put your bike in one of the barns to keep it out of the weather. It's just started snowing.'

'You got back to it all right?' Jessica asked.

'Yeah.' Henry frowned. 'As it happened, a motorist had stopped by it, and left his headlights on. It only took me a minute to get up there.'

'A motorist?'

'Yeah, I was a little surprised. To have two vehicles out this way at this time of night is quite a surprise. The guy had stopped to see if you needed any help, but looked a little concerned that the bike was unattended. I reassured him you were in a safe place and you'd be going on to your destination in the morning.'

Jessica frowned. 'He didn't happen to be wearing a hat and a trench coat, did he?'

Henry lifted an eyebrow. 'As a matter of fact, he did.'

12

BREAKFAST

JAMES TOOK THE TWO GIRLS TO A GUEST SUITE ON THE second floor, thankfully a Molly-free zone. Both girls were exhausted and within minutes were asleep on the room's comfortable twin beds. The next morning, feeling the most rested since her flat's pre-Doreen days, Jessica left Kirsten sleeping and headed down to see what had befallen her motorbike in the night.

The men were wandering across the courtyard, where a light snow had fallen overnight. Jessica realised she was completely unprepared for any kind of snow as it immediately engulfed the work boots in which she had ridden here. As she walked across to the covered barn where the men were now inspecting the Tomahawk, she felt the tickle of icy snow wetting her ankles.

'Quite a bike you've got here,' Henry said. 'I'd love something like this to take back to Hollydell, but unfortunately I'm on the sled. You be careful riding this in the snow.'

'You're leaving?'

'I'm afraid so. It's December 2nd. The season's kicking

off. You have a great time at Snowflake Lodge, and if you have a chance to get over to Hollydell to say hello, by all means.'

'Thank you.'

Out in the courtyard, she waited with James while Henry harnessed a couple of reindeer to a small sleigh. Then with a wave goodbye and a click of the reins, he was off down the lane and away.

'Breakfast?' James said, when Henry was out of sight. 'I've got fresh bread and cereal, coffee and orange juice. Better than you'd get in a Travel Lodge, I imagine.'

'I hope we're not imposing,' Jessica said, feeling suddenly awkward. 'We'll be on our way as soon as Kirsten wakes up.'

James shook his head. 'I didn't mean it like that. It's nice to have guests, even unexpected ones.'

Still unable to shake a sense that they were imposing, Jessica followed James inside. He had already laid out a table with some breakfast things.

'I have to say, you're an odd couple,' James said, pouring Jessica a cup of coffee out of a filter.

'She's my trainee,' Jessica said.

'Ah, I remember. You're a plumber with rich parents.' He grinned. 'Fantastic. I suppose if you have a decent safety net, you can try anything.'

'They're not my safety net,' she said, a little too sharply. 'Unlike my parents, I didn't want to spend my life sponging off my family fortune, not bothering to get a job, using their money, living in their house—'

James lifted an eyebrow. 'No, of course not. That would be terrible, wouldn't it?'

'Oh. Sorry. I didn't mean—'

'It's okay,' James said. 'I pay the mortgage. I had to remortgage the house to pay for my father's cancer treatment. He died in the end, but we had a couple of years together we might otherwise not have had. It was worth every penny, even if during the summer I work two jobs to keep up the payments.'

'I'm really sorry.'

James shrugged. 'Don't worry about it. I'm happy for you.'

Jessica wanted the ground to swallow her up. 'I'd better go and wake Kirsten. Then we'll be on our way. I can't thank you enough for helping us.'

'It was my pleasure.'

Jessica hurried upstairs, needing to get out of the conversation before she made things even worse. Perhaps it wasn't just Kirsten with a foot-in-mouth problem. The sooner they were out of James's house and back on the road the better.

Kirsten was still fast asleep. Jessica gave her a shake, then, while Kirsten was groggily sitting up in bed, went to the window and peered outside.

A perfect winter wonderland greeted her eyes. In the distance, tall mountains were topped with snow. Closer, rolling hills with forested valleys were blanketed with white, the road where they had come a line between two unblemished snowfields.

A car sat halfway along the road, angled so its driver's window was facing them.

Jessica narrowed her eyes. She had seen the car before, and even though it was too far away to make out the person sitting in the driver's seat, she knew without a doubt who it was.

Dick Burd.

'I've had enough of this,' she muttered, turning away from the window.

'Enough of what?' Kirsten mumbled, still half asleep

as she yawned. 'I don't think I could ever get enough of these beds.'

'I'll see you downstairs in a bit,' Jessica said, hurrying out of the room.

Downstairs, she ignored James, who was cooking bacon and eggs in the kitchen. She pulled on her coat and zipped it up, then headed out into the snow.

The wind had got up, gusting flurries of snow around her, making her wish she'd brought something a little more appropriate to wear than the old duffel jacket she wore for evening appointments. Also wishing she had a pair of thicker gloves, she stuffed her hands into her pockets and staggered down the lane to the road, somehow managing to avoid slipping over on several frozen puddles hidden under the fresh snowfall.

The lane dipped into a valley before crossing the railway line, for a few minutes putting Dick Burd's car out of sight. When it came back in sight, as Jessica climbed up the hill on the other side of the train tracks, he was no longer in the car, but outside of it, near to the stone wall bordering the road from the moorland beyond. And he was no longer alone.

Two old ladies, one walking a hardy sheepdog, had paused beside Dick Burd, who appeared to be picking stones up out of the snow and replacing them on the wall.

'What a thoughtful young man you are,' one of the women was saying as Jessica came into earshot. 'My Bob wouldn't be seen dead out here in this weather. And you can be quite sure none of the ruffians in the village would, either. I expect your parents are very proud of you.'

'I'm just thinking about the wildlife,' Dick Burd said. 'If a deer jumped over this wall into the path of a motorist, it might leave its babies without a parent.'

'Oh, what a thought!' the second woman exclaimed.

'Not to mention the danger to motorists,' Dick Burd continued. 'Who wants to have a traffic accident this close to Christmas?'

'Quite, quite,' the first woman said. 'Are you a local? I have a mind to put your name down for a community award.'

Dick Burd shook his head. 'No, I'm just travelling through,' he said.

'Well, before you go much further, you come over to Dotty here's house for some cookies and hot chocy,' the second woman said.

'Don't mind if I do,' said Dick Burd, standing up and brushing snow off his hands.

'Oh, my!' said the first woman. 'Don't you have any gloves? Your fingers will fall right off.'

'I saw the break in the wall and I just couldn't pass by without doing something,' Dick Burd said.

The women had each taken hold of one of Dick Burd's hands and were giving them a rub. Jessica retreated back down the road before she could either scream or vomit.

Kirsten was sitting at the dining room table eating breakfast when Jessica came in.

'… and once I get my NVQ, I'll be able to strike out on my own,' Kirsten was saying to James, who, nodding as he cupped his face with his hands, looked far more attentive than Kirsten's explanation probably deserved. 'But I'm hoping Ms. Lemond—I mean, Jessica—will take me on as a partner. Her firm has such a good reputation in the Bristol area. It would be a real boon to be involved.' Then, with a sudden animated wave of her hands, Kirsten added, 'No pipe is too old to be cleaned!'

'Really?' James said, raising an eyebrow.

'The TV ad is on YouTube,' Kirsten said. 'It's my favourite.'

Jessica grimaced as she hung up her coat and pulled off her boots. 'I retired it,' she said. 'If you read the comments on the video you'll see why.'

'But it did help with business, didn't it?'

Jessica nodded. 'Oh, yeah. I've never had so many calls. A shame most of them were from geriatric perverts.'

James shrugged. 'I suppose when you make a promise like that....' He laughed at Jessica's scowl. 'Nice walk? I heard you go out.'

'I wanted to have a word with the man who's been following me,' she said. 'The man in the car out on the road.'

'He was there first thing this morning,' James said. 'Is he stalking you? Do you want me to call the police?'

Kirsten was watching Jessica over the top of her spectacles as she crunched on a piece of toast. James wore a little smile, which while cute, made Jessica feel a little angry, as though he didn't take the situation seriously. But then, when she thought about it, it was ridiculous, after all. Dick Burd was trailing her in order to find her grandfather, and supposedly bring him to justice. Perhaps it was time to find Grandpa, get his side of the story once and for all, and get Dick Burd off their case. Send him out into the cold Scottish night with a souvenir bottle of Scotch whisky for Mavis Johns's bitter, money-grabbing family and a belly full of mince pies.

'No, it's okay,' Jessica said. 'I can handle it. He's harmless, just kind of annoying.'

James smiled. 'Well, how about we throw him off your tail? You're going to Snowflake Lodge, right? Well, the quickest way is to go back down via the road, but the most interesting way is along the forest path that leads up the valley from my farm. No way a car could ever make it, but your bike would be fine. It might get a bit muddy, but that's all.'

Jessica smiled. 'That sounds like a great idea.'

James nodded. 'But, you promised to do something for me first. Don't you remember?'

As Jessica was frowning, trying to remember last night's conversation, Kirsten jumped up out of the chair, both arms in the air, like a jack-in-the-box opened on Christmas Day.

'Decorate the Christmas tree!' she shouted.

13

SNOWFLAKE LODGE

'OKAY, READY EVERYONE? STAND BACK.'

James took a couple of steps back from the tree, Jessica and Kirsten on either side of him, then lifted a pair of wires in his hands.

'Ready? Three ... two ... one—'

'Merry Christmas!' they all shouted as the lights on James's tree came on, brightening the courtyard under a gloomy sky which threatened more snow. Even the cat, Molly, had come to the window to watch.

'That's an incredible tree,' Jessica said, staring up at the stunningly decorated pine tree rising several feet over her head. 'I could almost believe you built the farm around it.'

James smiled. 'Not quite. These pines grow pretty quick. The first Christmas after I took over the farm from my parents was quite a somber affair. That spring I broke a hole in the concrete and planted this tree. In the summer I ring it with flowers.'

'It's lovely,' Kirsten said. 'My family always made do with a plastic one out of Tesco. How about you?'

Jessica sighed. 'We had one of those glowing ones you

didn't need to decorate,' she said. 'My parents weren't into decorating all that much, not when you could get a tree that came ready. They liked to change it up, though, so they bought a new one every year.'

'It's all right for some,' James said, then immediately looked bashful. 'Sorry about that, I didn't mean—'

Jessica shrugged it off, but the damage had been done. She was the rich kid. As always, once people found out, it became something from which she had no escape. Not that it mattered; after all, he was a complete stranger. But, she liked the way he looked at her—

'It's starting to snow,' Kirsten said, tugging on Jessica's arm like a child who had forgotten her coat. 'I think we should get moving, don't you?'

To Jessica's disappointment—although she refused to say it out loud, nor even think it—James had no plans to accompany them on their onward journey. He explained that the reindeer needed feeding and cleaning before being taken out into the field for some exercise. He also needed to continue his checking of the fences in order to ensure none could get out like Belinda had the night before.

'You'll be fine,' he said, showing none of the disappointment that Jessica had secretly hoped to see. 'It's only narrow for the first couple of hundred metres. Then it widens out into a proper road. Another half a mile and you'll join up with the main road that heads up to Snowflake Lodge. Look out for the gapers on the top of the hill. It's the only spot for miles where you can pick up a phone signal. There's always a bunch of saddos up there holding their phones in the air, trying to pick up the latest social media stuff.'

'Are you not into all that?' Kirsten asked.

'Not when there's fresh air to breathe,' James said, sounding a little bitter. 'If people want to spend their lives staring at a phone, that's up to them. Personally, I'd rather live my life.'

The sudden vehemence with which he gave his opinion made their parting a little awkward. Jessica had been wondering whether to call Doreen and check that she still had a flat, but the reception blackspot had made the decision for her. She hadn't felt comfortable asking James if he had wi-fi, but Kirsten had figured it out by trying her phone and finding no roaming signals. As they climbed back onto the bike in the farm's courtyard, Jessica wasn't sure whether she was sad to be leaving or not.

'Good luck up at Snowflake Lodge,' James said. 'You'll have a great time.'

'Thanks for looking after us,' Kirsten said as she climbed into the sidecar, but all Jessica could do was mumble a quick thanks and flash a reluctant smile. Then they were off, and it felt easier not to look back. By the time she did allow herself to look in the wing mirror, the farm and James were out of sight.

The trail turned out as James had said. The bike bumped over the uneven ground for a couple of minutes, leaving a trail behind them in the snow, before the way opened out on to a proper forest lane. It wound beneath trees for a few minutes, in many places still clear of snow, then ended at a gate which opened onto the road.

A few minutes later they were surrounded by stunning mountain scenery: snow-peaked mountains, forested valleys, the occasional glitter of a distant lake between the hills. They passed a sign to Snowflake Lodge, then crested a hill where they found a small viewing layby filled with cars. Remembering James's words, Jessica's phone began to ping with all the messages it had been unable to collect during their time at James's place. She felt an urge to pull over and check, but resisted it. After a few minutes, the urge began to fade, she began to enjoy the scenery once more, and she wondered what all the fuss had been about.

At the top of the next rise they paused, looking down into a valley thick with forest in the shadow of a tall, jagged mountain. A single ski-run cut across its slopes, disappearing into the trees before reemerging by a car park at the bottom.

And there, nestled among the trees, was Snowflake Lodge.

Jessica pulled the bike onto the side of the road and took off her helmet to get an unhindered look. Kirsten also took off her helmet and together they stared in wonder.

'Well, I think we've found it,' Jessica said.

'It looks like Cinderella's castle,' Kirsten said. 'Oh, wow.'

She was right. Although several wings of the lodge were hidden among trees, the central building was at least three storeys tall and had a tower on one corner with an ornate turret on top. She wondered if up close it would look tacky, like an amusement park, but from a distance it looked like the fairytale-perfect set of a Christmas movie.

They climbed back onto the bike and headed down the valley. The main road passed the lodge to the west but an ornate cast iron gate stood over an entrance road lined by snow-covered fir trees lit up with Christmas lights. They turned up the road, bumping over gravel, the road winding uphill, until the pine trees were backed by thicker, darker forest on both sides. A car park appeared ahead, scattered with snow-covered vehicles. Jessica pulled in, then spotted another sign labeled STAFF PARKING. A gravel track led around to a shady area at the lodge's rear. Jessica parked in a free space, killed the engine, then pulled off her helmet and turned to Kirsten.

'Why do I feel nervous?' she asked. 'We've made it at last.'

Kirsten rubbed her hands together. 'Should we bring our stuff in now, or leave it here?'

'Let's make sure they've got room for us first. We're a few days earlier than expected.'

They headed around the lodge's front. Wide lawns now dusted with snow spread out around them, dotted with small statues and trees. Each was decorated with Christmas lights, which, unlike those under the trees, were currently switched off. In the centre of the gardens was an enormous pine tree, easily thirty feet high, encircled by Christmas lights and with a huge, magnificent star at the top.

'How delightful,' Kirsten said. 'I bet it looks even better at night.'

The main reception was at the top of a flight of steps. Off to the right was a wide courtyard patio in front of a large dining hall. Steps led down to the gardens below. Turning to take it all in, Jessica found herself gasping at the breadth of the panorama, the mountain rising over them, the snow-covered forest on the hillside below, the rolling moorland in the distance. It was so beautiful she could hardly bring herself to speak.

She glanced at Kirsten, gave a wordless nod and then pushed through the front door.

At the reception desk, a woman in her fifties—and dressed like she had time-travelled from the nineteen-fifties —was talking on the phone, a Christmas hat in her hands. Off to the left was a waiting area, currently empty. Comfortable sofas and armchairs made a semi-circle around a blazing log fire. On the mantelpiece above it, dclightfully colourful Christmas stockings hung down, and large, intricate snow globes reflected the ceiling lights.

Doors to the right led through into the dining room. As Jessica and Kirsten waited for the receptionist to finish her phone call, a rotund man in a bowler hat with a Christmas hat perched on top came bustling through, a clipboard under one arm, a single strand of hair flapping against the side of his face.

'Mildred?' he said, in a cartoonish harrumph voice which made Jessica smile. 'Mildred, are you still on hold? Can't they get someone out this afternoon? It's an emergency. How can we run a lodge with a blocked downstairs toilet?'

'Excuse me,' Jessica said, raising a hand like a nervous school kid uncertain of the correctness of her answer.

The man stopped. He turned, planted hands on hips with the power of someone claiming an overseas territory, then frowned.

'Guests must sign in at reception,' he said. 'The reception, as you can see right now, is busy, so if you don't mind waiting, there are some magazines over there in the lobby, and a pretty fish tank you can look at.'

'I like fish,' Kirsten said, as the man gave a dismissive harrumph and turned to face Mildred.

Jessica still had a hand in the air. 'Um, I'm Jessica Lemond. I'm the new plumber...? I'm a few days early, but—'

The man turned to face them. His cheeks had reddened as though he had been hitting the sherry a little too hard, but otherwise nothing in his expression had changed.

'The plumber, you say? Well what are you standing there for? Get your overalls on. This is an *emergency!*'

14

GRANDPA

Far from the emergency the rather tempestuous manager had proclaimed, the problem was actually a pretty simple one of a blocked U-bend. Jessica and Kirsten got to work on the problem, quickly identifying the location of the blockage, shutting down the water system and then removing, clearing, and replacing the offending section of pipe.

When he gave the toilet a confirming flush, the manager—whose name, rather fittingly, was Barry Trumpton—began clapping, joined by Mildred from reception who had accompanied them to the problematic cubicle.

'I can't thank you enough,' Barry said, turning to Jessica and Kirsten, his hands clasped together as though in prayer. 'That toilet has been playing up for years. All it takes is a little too much paper and we're flooded.'

'From what I've seen of it, the whole system is outdated,' Jessica said. 'The pipes are old, too thin for an establishment this size, and you have huge calcium deposits. Not to mention several fissures, most likely due to frost. I would suggest you get the whole lot overhauled during the off-season.'

Barry rolled his eyes. 'Try telling that to the mighty financers,' he said. 'Everything you say falls on deaf ears. The almighty conglomerate doesn't care about us. I really appreciate your help. If you can just get us through this season, I'll be eternally grateful.'

Mildred, all horn-rimmed spectacles, floral dress and exquisite bee-hive hair she refused to ruin with the Christmas hat held in her hands, leaned over Barry's shoulder.

'Um, Mr. Trumpton, the girls still haven't signed in yet. I imagine they've had a long drive.'

'We actually stayed locally last night,' Jessica said. 'With a local farmer? Um, James…?'

'James Wilcox?' Mildred said. 'Oh, you lucky girls. Both of you? Gosh, he's such a Casanova.'

'In the spare room,' Kirsten said quickly, her cheeks glowing like strawberries, eyes so wide at the thought of any innuendo that it made Jessica smile.

'We ran out of petrol,' she said.

'That Wilcox man is nothing but trouble,' Barry said. 'Never showing up on time—'

'He runs the sleigh rides,' Mildred said with a cheeky smile. 'They start next week. We posted a picture of him on the website last year and we had double the number of bookings from ladies over fifty.'

'And they caused so much trouble I had you take that picture down,' Barry said with a frown. 'I've never seen people drink so much wine spritzer.'

'He's not that handsome,' Jessica said, although in a way, he was. In a rugged, mountainous way. Not the kind of way she really liked, and in any case, his personality had been a little too spiky for her tastes.

'If you say so,' Mildred said, giving a subtle roll of her eyes. 'Come on, let's get you to your rooms.'

Jessica sighed, thinking about the panoramas she had seen from the main entrance. A cup of coffee—or even hot chocolate—and an armchair with a view would do nicely right now.

As though reading her thoughts, Kirsten said, 'Does our room have a view?'

Mildred grimaced. 'Kind of,' she said.

'Well, it's a view,' Kirsten said, sighing.

'Of the incinerator,' Jessica said, unable to resist a wry smile. The staff quarters, rather predictably, were at the building's rear, on a basement level, with a window that looked out onto a subterranean rubbish storage space. A large machine against the far wall looked capable of burning disgruntled guests, although when Jessica wiped a hand through the window's condensation to get a better look, she realised it was a giant industrial washing machine.

'At least we won't have to go far to wash our clothes,' Kirsten said.

Jessica sighed and pulled the curtains closed, covering the grim space outside with a pretty repeated scene of Father Christmas's North Pole grotto.

'Much better,' she said.

Other than the location, their shared suite was rather nice. They had a bedroom each, with a central room in the middle which doubled as a kitchen-diner. While Barry had given them staff coupons for the restaurant, they had the means to prepare and cook their own food if they wished.

'So what do we do now?' Kirsten asked.

'I suppose we'd better go and report for duty,' Jessica said. 'Don't forget your Christmas hat.'

Barry had explained—with a frustrated glance at Mildred, who was refusing to comply—that staff were required to wear Christmas hats at all times. With the heaters on only in the rooms, Jessica didn't really mind having something to keep her ears warm, even if Kirsten kept hers outside the hat like some kind of elf.

'I wonder what they'll want us to do?' Kirsten said, as they headed upstairs.

'Could be anything,' Jessica said.

The job description was "plumbing and general maintenance". When asked to clarify what exactly the "general maintenance" part entailed, Barry had shrugged. 'Just hang around in case we need you. And if it starts dumping with snow, grab a shovel and help out.'

Upstairs in reception, Mildred was polishing her nails, a magazine open on the desk in front of her. 'Did you settle in all right?' she asked. 'Sorry about the basement room. They're bigger than all the others, though. There is that.'

'It's fine,' Jessica said. 'I just had a couple of questions.'

Mildred shrugged, briefly taking her eyes off the magazine in order to look up. 'Sure, go ahead.'

'Is there anything we should be doing between maintenance jobs? Like, do we have an office we're supposed to hang out in, or is there anything covered by "general maintenance" that we should be getting on with?'

Mildred shook her head. 'Nope. Barry just likes to have someone on staff in case of an emergency. This place is sixty years old, and it's miles from anywhere. If something goes wrong it can take days to get fixed, especially if it's snowing. You're one of our little luxuries, but if you want something to do, just wander about and enjoy yourselves. The lodge has some lovely features and there are some great things to do outdoors. We've got that little ski slope, of course, but there are loads of forest trails, hikes, snowshoeing trips, ice fishing up at the mountain lake, not to mention all the Christmas events we have in the evenings. We're very much a community here, with a lot of the same customers every year. And of course, this year we have a very special guest on a farewell tour.'

Jessica gave a wry smile. 'That's something else I wanted to ask you about. Do you know where I could find my grandfather?'

Mildred laughed. 'Ah, I remember hearing that you were related to Ernest Lemond. It must be wonderful to have a famous family member.'

'It has its ups and downs, for sure,' Jessica said. 'Is he around somewhere? I haven't seen him since we arrived and I'd like to know how he's doing.'

'Oh, he's out on a trek,' Mildred said. 'He's gone up to the hot spring with a group of other guests.'

'A hot spring?'

Mildred grinned. 'Yes. The only one in Scotland. Isn't it great?'

'A trek?'

'Oh, it's only an hour or so up through the forest to the plateau. You should go. The views are fantastic.' She winked. 'And you can get phone reception.'

Jessica glanced at Kirsten, who gave a little shrug. 'That's all well and good,' she said to Mildred, 'but my grandfather is ninety-two. Ninety-three in February.'

'I know, amazing isn't it?' Mildred said. 'That's the thing about Snowflake Lodge. A little time here takes years off you. Makes you feel young again. You wouldn't think he was a day over eighty.'

Kirsten tugged on Jessica's sleeve. 'Won't that be good? You can put off thirty for a few more years.'

Jessica grimaced, shrugged Kirsten off like a clingy child and looked back at Mildred. 'Well, that's nice, but I think it's time I went and found him.'

With Kirsten trailing along behind, they did a quick reconnaissance mission of the hotel, getting familiar with its layout. A large dining room was cozier than something its size ought to have been, with two log fires burning on either side of the doors to the kitchens, while in the centre was a large Christmas tree surrounded by presents, which gave the impression the room was far smaller than it really was.

Through a door on the other side was a quaint souvenir shop, some function rooms set up for Christmas activities such as cooking and decoration-making, then a rental shop for ski and hiking gear. All the guest rooms were either above them on the first and second floors, or behind them, in disconnected cabins built on steps in the hillside and accessed via covered stairways that led up through the forest.

Past the rental shop was a door that led outside, into a side courtyard from where numerous small roads and paths led away. One way led directly uphill to the ski slope behind the hotel, while others had signs indicating nature trails and hikes.

'Are you up for a forest walk?' Jessica said, glancing back, but to her surprise Kirsten was no longer behind her. She wandered back a little way and found the younger girl standing by a rack of books in the souvenir shop.

'Kirsten? I'm going to take a hike up to this hot spring,' Jessica said. 'Do you want to come?'

Kirsten looked up. 'I think, if it's all right by you, I'll let you have a little family time,' she said. Then, holding up a generic thriller which was too far away for Jessica to even read the title, Kirsten added, 'I've always wanted to read this one.'

'Sure, no problem.'

Jessica headed for the door. As soon as she stepped outside, she realised she was in no way dressed for a winter mountain hike. She went back inside to the rental shop, where a teenage boy in a Christmas hat lent her an insulated ski jacket, boots, and gloves.

Suitably attired, Jessica headed outside. A clear blue sky gave plenty of light as she followed the path into the trees. A light dusting of snow covered the ground, but just in case the path got buried, markers topped with red tape were positioned every few steps to indicate the correct way to go.

Under the trees, the air turned quickly cold, but in the pristine pine forest Jessica felt a peace unlike any she could remember. Within a few minutes she was out of range of the tinkling music playing from speakers on the hotel's walls, and all she could hear was the creak of branches and the drip of melting snow.

She had brought her phone, and remembered the pings of delivered messages she had picked up on the approach road to the lodge. She felt a sudden urge to check but suppressed it. Whatever it was could wait. It would only spoil the mood of this place. Stopping and closing her eyes for a moment, Jessica breathed in the scent of the pine forest, letting the stillness engulf her senses.

Carrying on, the path quickly began to steepen. She

reached a fork, with a sign pointing off to the left indicating FISHING LAKE. The one continuing up said:

HOT SPRING
VIEWING SPOT
MOUNTAIN PEAK
This Way
(It's not far, promise!)

Jessica, whose thighs were beginning to ache, paused to take a breath. As she started off again, from further up the path came the sound of laughter.

And not just any laughter, but a shrill titter which had once been a stable of Saturday night television.

'And remember,' came a joyous voice at which Jessica couldn't stop herself smiling, 'when life gives you lemons, suck on an orange.'

She increased her pace, passing one viewing spot with a wonderful panorama of the surrounding hills. The laughter was close by, though, so she urged her aching legs onwards, until the trees began to part above her. She emerged into a clearing, where she immediately became disorientated because of the mist billowing across the path up ahead. Then she realised it wasn't actually mist but steam, rising from a natural rock pool a little way further ahead. Towels were draped over a couple of wooden benches, alongside piles of clothes. Someone had put a Christmas hat on top of one. Beside it was a flask made out of wood and a packet of paper cups.

Jessica was still staring at the cups when a voice hailed her out of the steam.

'Oh my dilly dally days, is that my granddaughter? Jessica, dear, is that you?'

A shape moved amongst the steam, a person, standing

up out of the water. Jessica had only a moment to avert her eyes before her grandfather's skeletal, near-naked form appeared. He held a tiny hand towel over his nether regions, not that it made much difference. Jessica would never be able to look at a plucked turkey the same way again.

'Hi, Grandpa,' Jessica said, thankful as he lowered himself back into the water. 'It's nice to see you again.' *Although I could handle seeing a little less.*

'Dear, I heard you'd got yourself a job up here at the lodge. Such a wonderful place, don't you agree? Why don't you strip off and jump on in? The breeze will blow the steam off in minutes and you'll get a look at the view. It's magnificent. Like being on top of the world.'

'Um, I didn't bring a swimsuit.'

'Oh, don't be a silly thing. You don't need a suit. We're all starkers in here.'

Jessica grimaced and averted her eyes as Grandpa stood up again to prove his point, waving his bony arms in the air. Thankfully the steam was thick enough around the water's edge to cover the parts she least wanted to see, but Jessica made a point of looking away, up at the mountain peak rising a few hundred metres above them as the wind blew the steam aside.

Then, from behind Grandpa came a couple of giggles. Jessica really didn't want to see who was in there with him, but the wind disagreed, blowing aside the steam with a sudden hard gust to reveal two middle-aged ladies sitting on the other side of the hot spring.

'Hello,' Jessica said, giving the two ladies a shy smile.

'Hello, love.'

'Hello, deary.'

'How rude of me,' Grandpa said, regrettably jumping up again, then covering his mouth with his hands in a dramatic gesture that was right out of his TV heyday. 'Let me introduce you to my friends. On the left is Demelza from the kitchen, and on the right, from housekeeping services, is Charity.'

As the two ladies began to laugh along with him, Jessica wondered just how volcanic the area might be to have produced a hot spring, and whether, if she prayed really, really hard, the mountain might just open a quick fissure to swallow her right up.

15

TEAM MEETING

WHILE THE THOUGHT OF SITTING IN A NATURAL BATH OF hot water while looking at a panoramic view of the Scottish Highlands really quite appealed, Jessica wasn't in the mood for company, particularly when it came with a heavy dose of innuendo. She bid her grandfather and his companions farewell and headed back down the path to the lodge.

Kirsten was nowhere to be found in the reception area, so Jessica grabbed a cup of complimentary hot chocolate from a table in the dining room and found a comfortable armchair near one of the open fires. There were a selection of books and magazines in a rack beside the chair, but she couldn't resist pulling out her phone. Somehow she knew it was going to be bad news, and she was right.

Get on, Lemons, Doreen's message began. *I hope you're enjoying the holiday while neglecting your landlord duties. Should have expected it—easy life for you rich kids, isn't it? Thought I'd better let you know that the light fitting in the kitchen's gone. Phil got a bit excited when the sports news said the Gunners are selling Pascoe to*

Millwall, but it was just a tap. The thing just popped off. We're cooking by torchlight at the moment. Any chance you can get someone round? This place is a death trap. It'll be unlivable soon.

Jessica felt a knot of anger building up inside. She started to type a reply, before realising she had no phone connection. She held her phone above her head, waving it back and forth, hoping just to get a couple of bars of signal, enough to tell Doreen that she was the kind of nightmare who made Krampus look like a welcome friend. She had just let out a wail of anger when she caught sight of a figure walking past the window. Wearing a duffel coat with the hood up, he had only briefly turned in her direction, but she had caught the look in his eyes as the lights from the dining room illuminated his face.

James Wilcox. And the way he had looked at her had been how Father Christmas might have looked at a naughty child.

No presents for you this year.

She felt a sudden urge to tell him she wasn't addicted to her mobile phone like it might seem, but by the time she had reached the side door by the rental shop, there was no sign of him.

Frustrated, she went to reception where Mildred was reading a magazine about 1950s bicycles.

'Um, hi, I was just wondering if James Wilcox was working here today?'

Mildred smiled. 'Oh, wouldn't we all be so lucky?'

Jessica felt herself blushing. 'I just thought I saw him, and you said he does the sleigh rides—'

'They're not due to start until next week,' Mildred said, running her finger down a ledger book. 'No, he's not supposed to be in today.'

Jessica grimaced. 'Perhaps I was mistaken.' *Or perhaps I'm losing my mind.*

She thanked Mildred and headed back to her spot by the fire, but now it had been taken by a group of skiers fresh off the slope, their skis propped up in front of the fire while they sipped from cans of beer. Instead, Jessica headed back to her room for a lie down.

That evening Barry called a staff meeting. Jessica had spent the afternoon asleep while Kirsten had apparently found a small library for customer use on the second floor, where she had spent the rest of the afternoon. As they followed other workers into a function room to the right of the reception, Jessica looked around for Grandpa, but he was nowhere to be seen.

Barry climbed up onto a chair—rather precariously, considering his ample size—and clapped his hands together.

'All right, you lot, thanks for showing up at short notice,' he said, clearing his throat with a quick, customary harrumph. 'We have two new members of staff joining us today on the general maintenance team. Jessica and Kirsten. Welcome, ladies. It's a pleasure to have you here.'

He waved a hand in their direction, and the entire group turned and began to applaud. Jessica's cheeks burned, while Kirsten ducked behind her shoulder like a frightened rabbit.

'Thanks for joining us,' Barry said again. 'If you have any questions, please ask one of us. We run a tight but pretty relaxed ship here at Snowflake Lodge. As long as the job gets done, it's okay to have fun. Happy staff make for happy customers, and as long as the customers are happy, the conglomerate will be happy too.'

The conglomerate. It was the second time he had

mentioned it. Jessica had seen no corporate logos anywhere, so she presumed whichever massive multinational company was running Snowflake Lodge, it was staying in the background.

'A few words please,' Barry said, waving at Jessica.

Kirsten, her hands squeezing Jessica's arm, was visibly shaking. Jessica didn't feel much better, but she forced a smile and looked around at all the beaming faces. In fact, everyone except Barry wore a huge grin. Both her grandfather's companions—Demelza from the kitchen and Charity from housekeeping—were there, although fully clothed this time, and she recognised the young man from the rental shop.

'Thanks,' she croaked. 'We're happy to be here. If you have a blocked toilet or sink, give us a shout.'

The crowd clapped as though she'd just made a speech worthy of the history books. As people patted her arms and reached out to shake both hers and Kirsten's hands, Barry clapped his hands for order again.

'I'd like to remind everyone of the rules,' he said, still standing on the chair. 'And I'd also like to remind everyone that they are not my rules, but the conglomerate's rules, so there's no use complaining to me if you don't like them. Christmas hats should be worn at all times.' He gave Mildred a pointed glare. The receptionist scowled back at him, lifted her hat and hooked it over one ear. 'A cup of hot chocolate—or, if off-duty but in the communal areas, a glass of sherry, although fruit punch is acceptable for the non-drinkers—should be within arms' reach at all times. There are three hot chocolate stations within the communal areas that are filled up hourly, so you have no excuse. Christmas songs should be hummed or sung— whistling is also allowed—whenever you are within earshot of a customer. All off-duty staff members are required to wear a Christmas sweater: as cheesy as possible. If you haven't yet purchased one, there are many available in the souvenir shop at a huge staff discount, so you have no excuse. And finally, on karaoke nights, no staff member is allowed to refuse a customer request. Is that clear?'

A cheer rose up from the crowd, as though they were very clear on the rules. In fact, only Barry looked unhappy about them.

'See you in the bar, Trumpers!' someone shouted. 'Looking forward to this year's rendition of the Chicken Song!'

The scowl on Barry's face as he looked around for the heckler was telling, but whoever it was, they were now keeping their head down.

'I ask you that you respect the conglomerate's rules,' he said, then clapped his hands together. 'Meeting over.'

The staff filed out. A few people stayed behind to congratulate Jessica and Kirsten on joining the team, but within a minute they were left standing alone with Barry, who had removed his Christmas hat and the bowler underneath and was in the process of rearranging what was left of his hair.

'Ghastly things,' he said, holding the Christmas hat out in front of him like he might a dead mouse. 'I'll be pleased when the season's over.'

'You're not a fan of Christmas?' Jessica asked.

Barry rolled his eyes. 'All these lights and shiny things, and people being silly all the time … gets in the way of your day, don't you think?'

Jessica just shrugged. 'I suppose it might.'

'I love Christmas,' Kirsten said, the Christmas hat pulled so far down over her hair that Jessica could only just see her eyes.

'Whatever tickles your fancy,' Barry said, turning to

glare at a Christmas hat someone had left hanging on the back of a chair. 'Mildred,' he said, rolling his eyes. 'She'll be the death of me if the conglomerate finds out.'

'What exactly is the conglomerate?' Jessica asked.

Barry shook his head. 'You don't want to know.'

He grabbed Mildred's discarded hat and headed for the door, but Jessica stopped him with a sharp, 'Wait!'

'What is it? If there's anything else, you can ask that fair-weather on the reception desk.'

'Um, do you know where I can find my grandfather?'

Barry rolled his eyes. 'Our resident celebrity? That would be in the executive suite.'

'Where's that?'

'The tower room. On the third floor. I imagine he's in there right now, hassling the staff for caviar and truffles. Poor old Charity, she's smitten with that old dinosaur. Do you think if I asked Father Christmas for a meteor aimed right at us this Christmas, he might oblige for once?'

Jessica was left speechless as Barry swung Mildred's hat over his shoulder like a skinned mink and marched out, switching the lights off on the way, only remembering to leave the door open as an afterthought with a sharp harrumph.

'Well, I guess he told us,' Jessica said, glancing at Kirsten's silhouette.

'It was interesting, don't you think?' Kirsten said.

'What?'

'A fair-weather. I've never heard that before. Is that Dickensian?'

For the second time in the space of a couple of minutes, Jessica was left speechless.

16

LIFE ADVICE

JESSICA FELT LIKE A CRAZED FAN AS SHE LIFTED A HAND to knock on the door of her grandfather's suite. The old timer, due to perform next Saturday, had kept a low profile in the few days since Jessica's arrival. She had caught the occasional fleeting glimpse at the far end of corridors and once even found him in the dining room, surrounded by a giggling entourage of elderly ladies, only to have Mildred tug on her arm and pull her away to an urgent blocked toilet before she was able to speak to him.

This was the seventh attempt to speak to him in his room. Three times he had been out somewhere, twice sleeping, and twice "engaged". Jessica had promised her parents she would check up on him, but she was nearly ready to pack her bags and head back to Bristol before Doreen demolished her flat.

Knock. 'Please…' Knock. '…answer…' Knock. '…your—'

The door flew open. Rather than one of her grandfather's "maids", as Jessica had taken to calling them, to her surprise it was the old man himself. Up close he looked every bit of his ninety-two years, more wrinkles and liver spots than features, but through it all shone the wide eyes, the cheeky smile, and even the hideous light-brown toupee which had made him a darling of Saturday night TV for several decades.

'Oh, Jessica, darling, there you are. I've been looking everywhere for you.'

'Really? *You've* been looking for *me?*'

'I've had scouts all over. Like ants to carry you home. None have yet. Have you put on weight?' He gave a tittering laugh, then patted a stomach that Jessica considered yoga-trained flat, even if her only yoga poses were squeezing into awkward spaces beneath sinks.

'About twenty stone,' Jessica said. 'At least since you last paid me any attention.'

Grandpa laughed again. 'Oh, you jest. A chip off the old block, you are. Or should I say a slice off the old marshmallow?'

Jessica had a sudden flashback to her childhood, of sitting on Grandpa's knee and watching cartoons while stuffing marshmallows and hot chocolate into their mouths. Her parents had been off on some overseas tour, and Grandpa, fresh from professional retirement, had taken it upon himself to get to know his grandchild a little better.

They had been wonderful days, full of laughter and fun.

'I've missed you, Grandpa,' she said, a tear beading in the corner of her eye as she pulled the old man into a hug. 'I've hardly seen you these last ten years or so.'

Grandpa's bony hands patted her on the shoulders, then Jessica helped him to a chair, the sprightliness that had somehow got him up to the hot spring impossible to see. For ninety-two, he looked in remarkable shape, his body not bowed by age like so many older people, but age was age. If she did even half what he had done in his life by the time she was done, she would be happy.

'Would you like a drink?' Jessica asked.

'Oh, yes please. I'm afraid I gave the maids the afternoon off. There were a couple of movies I wanted to watch, but the TV was on the blink, so I took a nap, then went over a little old material for next week's show.'

Grandpa had certainly been given the best view in the hotel. Three large, connected rooms all had wide, floor-to-ceiling windows giving a panoramic view of the moorland rolling away. It had begun to snow again, the scene reminding Jessica of the flying section of *The Snowman*, when Peter Auty sang *Walking in the Air* while James and the Snowman flew over the snow-covered fields.

'Mine's the sugar-free light hot chocolate,' Grandpa said. 'I don't have the constitution I once had. I imagine it's my fault you have so much work to do.'

Jessica grimaced. 'Thanks, Grandpa. I didn't need to know that.'

She made hot chocolate for Grandpa and coffee for herself, adding a couple of sugar-free marshmallows to his saucer, and a few full fat beauties to hers—presumably ones he kept for his maids. He had taken an armchair near to the window, so Jessica pulled another beside him, a little table between them on which she put their drinks.

'So, what happened, Grandpa?'

He lifted an eyebrow. 'Why the vanishing act? You see, my dear, I'm ninety-two. Much as I'd be happy to live forever, it's quite likely I'll be done in a year or two. Wouldn't mind my telegram from the Queen—I do wonder if she'll use lemon-coloured paper?—but I'd settle for six months of fun over a few years in a nursing home. I quite passed the burn-out-not-fade-away moment about six decades ago, but it's not too late to go out on my sword, is it?'

Jessica smiled. 'I meant, what happened with Mavis?'

'With that dragon?' Grandpa leaned forward, skeletal hands gripping the arms of the chair. He lifted one eyebrow while simultaneously reducing the other eye to a slit, then wrinkled what was left of his nose as he said, 'Are you worried that I … *murdered* her? That I crept up behind her and gave her ladder a quick shake while she wasn't looking, then snuck back indoors and pretended to sleep in my chair until I was awoken by the neighbour's shouting? Because it would only have taken a minute, wouldn't it? And that awful woman was always so wrapped up in her own thing that she wouldn't have noticed me in a million years, not even if I'd dressed up as a lemon and squawked like a bird.' He leaned even further forward, until Jessica thought he might fall out of the chair. 'Cluck? Cluck … cluck … *cluck?*'

'Um … you didn't, did you?'

Grandpa threw himself back in the chair so hard his back clicked. He burst into laughter, thumping the chair's armrests.

'Of course I didn't. I can barely get out of my chair without assistance. And that woman had locked the door from the outside, just to make sure I didn't wander off. I imagine the police ignored that one, didn't they?'

Jessica shook her head. 'I didn't know—'

'Figures. When life gives you lemons, and all that. Here I am, one of the greatest comedians of my generation, kept prisoner by my dead wife. Not something you want out in the papers, is it? Not when your son and daughter-in-law are off spending all your money.'

'Grandpa, I—'

He leaned forward again, his body creaking like the

bag of bones it resembled. 'It's not impossible that I paid someone to knock that old witch off … but she could easily have flown away!'

He burst into laughter again, leaving Jessica unsure whether he had been in the middle of a confession or a joke. Unsure quite what to say, she stuffed a marshmallow into her mouth and looked at the view until his cackling had subsided.

'I'm proud of you, Jessica,' he said suddenly. She looked at him, surprised, but there was no hint of a punchline to come. 'I'm proud because you've made something of yourself. Look at you, a business owner! You think I haven't had a look at your website? And that time you were on *Britain's Historic Homes*—'

Jessica rolled her eyes. 'I had one line,' she said. 'And it was BBC iPlayer. Only about thirty people watched it.'

'TV is TV,' Grandpa said. 'You're a chip off the old block. Not like my lay-about son. Do you think I got where I did in life by sitting around doing nothing? All you know is the T-shirts and the DVDs, and the legions of adoring fans.' He couldn't resist a little sigh of contentment, but then his eyes hardened once more. 'You know I fought in the war, don't you? France, 1945? Sure, it was almost over by the time I was sent out there, but I still saw action. And what I saw made me realise that if you have the chance to bring a smile to someone's face, you should do it. I spent the next fifteen years in the pubs and the basement clubs, sleeping in the back of a rundown old van, on a dirty mattress, under a blanket I sewed together from two old jackets. I earned nothing but applause in most of those places, but if anyone thinks I didn't earn my success, they have no idea.'

Jessica shook her head. 'No, I had no idea. Dad never talked about it.'

'That silly fool doesn't know,' Grandpa laughed. 'I was well established before he came along, and you know, no point looking back, is there? Sunrise is always brighter than sunset. Lemon-bright, some might say.' That twinkle again. 'Whatever people might think of a crusty ninety-two-year-old man enjoying his last few days—because let's face it, years is pushing it a bit—no one who knows me can say I haven't earned it. Because I have.' He leaned closer, back creaking. 'Although, whisper it, but those years I spent in filthy bars and clubs, being heckled off the stage, having drinks thrown over me, watching fights break out over jokes that were taken the wrong way … those were the best years. I enjoyed every minute of it. For every person who got the hump, there was someone who was dying with laughter, and a few of those were women. There were plenty of nights I wasn't alone on that dirty old mattress.'

He burst into laughter. Jessica just cringed, although she could sympathise, having been single for most of her twenties and with no sign of land on the horizon as she closed on thirty. After a couple of sherries, she would almost be prepared to jump into bed with Barry.

'I'm so glad to see you again, Grandpa,' she said. 'I hope you'll have time in your busy schedule to hang out with your little … Lemon.'

Grandpa smiled the most genuine smile he had yet. 'I loved every minute of babysitting you,' he said. 'You grew up far too fast.'

'And I'm getting old far too fast too.'

'Your dad said you didn't have a boyfriend,' Grandpa said. 'Or a girlfriend, if that's the way you swing.'

Jessica cringed. 'Boy is fine,' she said. 'And no, not currently.'

'Not for years, your dad said. He's worried he's not going to have a wedding to spend all my money on.'

'I'm not sure I could find a free date in between all their cruises,' Jessica said.

'Just don't invite them,' Grandpa said. 'I didn't invite my parents to my first wedding. Although we eloped, and I was sixteen. Gretna Green and all that. God, what times. We were married nine days before she had a change of heart and annulled it. Hadn't even done the deed.'

'That was your first marriage?'

Grandpa smiled. 'Oh, no, I don't even mention that one. It was more of a practice run. Honestly, all those biographies and they still haven't dug that one up yet. I wonder what all these writers get paid for? Sitting on their bums and surfing the internet, no doubt. But let's not talk about me. Let's talk about you.'

'I don't want to talk about me.'

'Sure you do. What about that lovely young lad who rents the snowboards?'

'He's a teenager!'

'Ah, he won't be for long. And you can enjoy his best years. You know, they say a man's libido peaks at eighteen. All downhill after that, unless you medicate.' He winked. 'Luckily I have good doctors.'

'Grandpa, please….'

'Well, who else is there? There's that puff of hot air who thinks he's running the place. We'll cross him off. He has the hots for that receptionist anyway.'

'Really?'

'You can see it a mile off. When you're looking back as far as me, at any rate. And she likes him, but she'd never admit it.'

'I'd never have thought.'

'Watch them together. That's what life's about, mostly. Watching. Really watching. You'll be amazed what you see if you only take the time to really look.'

'Okay, I'll try.'

Grandpa wrinkled his chin. 'So … who else is there?'

Jessica shifted uncomfortably. 'Perhaps I'd better let you get some rest—'

'Aha! The reindeer guy. Thomas? Simon? What's his name again?'

'James Wilcox.'

'Ah, so you remember. A sure sign that you're besotted.'

Jessica felt her cheeks reddening. 'What? I'm not—'

Grandpa leaned forward and patted her on the knee. 'It's okay to tell your old Grandpa, my little Lemon. Your secret is safe with me—'

The door opened, and two women came bustling in, carrying bags of shopping. Demelza from the kitchen and Charity from housekeeping. They stopped when they saw Jessica and began to back out.

'We're sorry, we didn't realise Mr. Lemond had company—'

'It's okay,' Jessica said, standing up. 'I need to get on. I'm supposed to be on duty in case any more pipes get blocked.' She turned to Grandpa. 'We'll talk again soon.'

Grandpa winked. 'We certainly will,' he said.

17

GAMES IN THE SNOW

JESSICA WENT BACK DOWNSTAIRS, CHECKING IN WITH Mildred at reception first to see if there was anything that needed doing. Mildred just shrugged and shook her head, so Jessica headed downstairs to her room.

Kirsten was nowhere about, but had left evidence that she had recently been in attendance—a coffee mug and a chocolate bar wrapper on the table, next to a book on the French Revolution which had a stamp on the front saying Snowflake Library.

Jessica made herself a drink and pulled a chair near to the window, looking out on the basement view, where someone had thoughtfully strung up some Christmas lights over the giant washing machine and even stuffed a rather forlorn Christmas tree in between a drying rack and a storage cupboard.

She was still buzzing from her conversation with Grandpa. In such a short space of time she had learned so much about him that she had never known, plus a little about herself. No, she didn't need a boyfriend, even if James's mockery of her had left her feeling more perturbed than it perhaps should have. Who was he to judge her anyway? It wasn't like he had a nightmare lodger destroying his property.

Almost by habit, Jessica pulled out her phone. A new message had appeared, perhaps one she had picked up while in Grandpa's suite on the third floor. She groaned as she opened it.

This place has become unlivable, Lemons. You should be ashamed of yourself. Last night the lock on the front door broke. The key was a little stiff because of the cold so all I did was give it a little shove. Not even angrily, more just miffed. And the whole thing popped out. You call this security? I'll be going to the letting agency in the morning. And if you think I'm paying next month's rent, you can forget it. Screw you, Lemons.

Jessica just sighed. With no way to reply, she just tossed her phone onto the floor and rubbed her eyes. Perhaps the lodge needed someone year round? She certainly felt no desire to go back when her contract was over.

Lemons.

How had a single letter made her grandfather's beloved childhood nickname for her become so hated? She had beamed every time he called her his little Lemon, but once secondary school kicked in and Lemons became her moniker, chanted in classrooms and shouted down hallways, she had despised everything about her family name. She had hated her family's money, reviled her famous connection. And left everything she loved about her family behind. Yet all along, it had been Grandpa who had led the kind of life to which she should aspire. A life where you just didn't give a damn.

She sat up. Screw men and lodgers from hell. It was time to take charge. She needed a drink. Alcohol would do, but hot chocolate would be better.

By the time she had walked upstairs, clear skies had given way to a curtain of falling snow. Guests and staff alike had gathered by the window to ooh and aah as the courtyard transformed into a polar playground. Jessica found Kirsten, a huge tome of European history clutched against her chest, standing near the door, peering through a circle someone had wiped in the condensation.

'Isn't it delightful?' Kirsten said by way of greeting, her cheeks flushed from something Jessica suspected was a lot stronger than hot chocolate. 'They're saying it'll be snowing like this for days.'

Before Jessica could reply, the sound of someone clapping came from the direction of reception. 'Shovels! Shovels! Shovels!' hollered Barry as he ran through the dining hall. 'We'll be snowed in! Everyone on duty, outside, now!'

Jessica joined the other staff as they hurried after Barry to the main doors. An old janitor she had learned was known only as Mr. Dawes because he refused to tell anyone his first name had pushed a wheelbarrow loaded with snow shovels up to the front doors. Jessica joined a queue and soon was merrily shoveling snow off the entrance steps. Used to the slushy, dirty gunk that was all she ever saw in Bristol, the snow was a revelation. She had never seen snow like it: so light and fluffy that most of every shovelful ended up cascading down around her.

They had been digging for about twenty minutes, with the mood slowly rising to the point where Christmas songs were being hummed all over the place, when suddenly someone lost in the mist of the snow shouted, 'Snowball fight!'

A chaos like Jessica had never known ensued. Amidst

much laughter, she found herself herded to one side of the car park with a blue scarf thrust into her hands.

'The flowerbed,' gasped the teenager from the snowboard rental shop. 'That's the fort.'

No other explanation seemed necessary. The blues surged forward, fluffy, disintegrating snowballs making little to no impact whatsoever on the group wearing orange scarves, who had climbed up on the wall of the car park's central flowerbed. Unsure quite what she was supposed to do other than heave snow about the place, Jessica joined in, only to catch a massive blow from the side which went right down her neck. She scooped up a handful and turned, scowling, only to see Kirsten, orange scarf around her neck and hands up, muttering 'Sorry! That wasn't meant for you!'

Jessica cocked to throw in any case, but then someone else shouted, 'To the tree! Group snow angel!'

Again unsure what was going on, Jessica dropped her snowball, took Kirsten by the arm instead, and together they followed the others through the snow towards the massive, snow covered poplar tree on the edge of the car park. The strings of Christmas lights that encircled its fifteen-metre height had been dulled by the snow, but someone had produced a thick rope, which was apparently tied to the tree about halfway up.

'All hands to the rope. Newbies under the tree!'

As Jessica led Kirsten under the nearest snow-laden branches, she wondered what was supposed to happen. When the same person shouted, 'Heave!' she twigged.

A massive cascade of fluffy snow rained down, coating them, and burying them up to the knees. Kirsten squealed with excitement. Jessica wiped snow off her face and turned to see Mr. Dawes, now wearing a Christmas hat, bellowing with laughter. Nearby, the teenager from the rental shop picked up a soccer ball sitting on top of the snow and exclaimed, 'I wondered where that went.'

'I can see why they call it Snowflake Lodge,' Kirsten said, gasping. 'I mean, there's a lot of snow, isn't there? Oh, hail Saint Nick and his eight mighty steeds!'

Jessica cringed, but before Kirsten's social goofing could embarrass her, a sharp crackle came out of the whiteness, and then Barry's amplified voice said, 'Stop mucking about, you lot. Get the car park and the drive clear. We have two buses from Silver Tours coming in this evening and I don't want them having to push wheelchairs up from the main road.'

Low moans of 'Scrooge, Scrooge,' the O's drawn out like a rugby chant, came from all around them. As Jessica followed the other revelers back to where they had left their shovels, she couldn't help but smile.

18

AN OLD JACKET

SILVER TOURS TURNED OUT TO BE A MISNOMER; ITS attendees leaning on the grey to balding side, as Jessica joined the rest of the staff to help a procession of elderly in wheelchairs or with walkers up the snow-laden disabled access path to the side of the main steps. Barry seemed terrified by the prospect of so many geriatric guests, but from the Christmas hats and the wide, delighted grins of the new arrivals, they shared none of his misgivings.

While they had been out in the snow, a huge cardboard cutout of Grandpa had appeared in the lobby, advertising his lodge debut on Saturday at seven o'clock. A huge line of chairs quickly formed for each of the geriatrics to get a photograph next to an image of their hero. Jessica, helping out, wondered why the old man himself couldn't make an appearance, but when she put the question to Mildred at reception, she was told that it was part of the mystery.

'Oh, and he's gone hiking.'

'What? It's four o'clock in the afternoon. It's dark outside!'

'You haven't seen the illumination trail, have you? It goes all the way up to this year's Yule tree.'

Jessica shook her head. 'No, I'm afraid I haven't.'

'The ceremonial cutting will take place on Sunday, but until then it's all lit up and decorated.' Mildred sighed. 'Very romantic. It's also a little steep, but if you wear proper shoes you'll be all right.'

'And Grandpa—I mean, Mr. Lemond—has gone up there? You do know he's ninety-two? He can barely walk without assistance.'

'Oh, he has assistance. We never let anyone go up there alone after dark without a staff member or a guide. Don't worry, he'll be fine. He bounces around like he's eighty, doesn't he?'

Jessica grimaced. 'That's one way of putting it.'

With nothing else going on except a loud discordant karaoke session in the dining room, Jessica made up her mind. She went off to find Kirsten, but the girl was not in their room. Eventually she located her in the rental shop, talking to the teenaged student.

'Kirsten, do you fancy a walk in the snow?' Jessica said, before realising from the student's body language that they had been about to engage in some sort of tryst. Backtracking, she said, 'Um, it's okay, I'll go on my own.'

Kirsten turned around, her cheeks flushed. The student had one arm on a rack of snowboarding jackets, his hand tantalizingly close to Kirsten's shoulder. Jessica felt like a total party pooper, but the student shrugged and told Kirsten he ought to get back to work.

'Sure,' Kirsten said, sounding crestfallen as she turned to Jessica. 'If you like.'

They pulled on jackets and boots they had left to dry by the side entrance, then set out. After they had gone a little way, Jessica said, 'Sorry about that. I didn't mean to interrupt.'

Kirsten shook her head. 'We were just chatting,' she said. 'His name is Ben. He goes to Edinburgh University, but they just broke up for the winter. He's into Haruki Murakami.'

'Who?'

'He's a Japanese magical realism novelist,' Kirsten said. '*Kafka on the Shore?*'

Jessica grimaced. 'I'm afraid I rarely get further than *Pipes and Spanners Monthly.*'

Kirsten whooped an embarrassingly loud laugh. A little upslope, a tree shuddered, releasing its load of snow. 'I imagine that's exciting in its own way.'

'Not so much. Anyway, sorry for interrupting.'

'You're the boss,' Kirsten said, making Jessica wince. While Kirsten meant it as a joke, it reminded Jessica of their status. She wished they could relax and be friends, but perhaps she had only invited Kirsten because she didn't have any real friends, something of which Doreen had taken pride in reminding her. *Hey, Lonely Lemons, we're going to the football game. You can come if you want. I mean, what else are you going to do? Talk to your hands? Chatty, are they?*

'I have friends,' she muttered out loud.

'I'm sorry?'

Jessica shook her head. 'Nothing. Come on, let's find this tree. It's freezing out here, isn't it?'

'But it's lovely at the same time. I keep expecting to see the Polar Express come rushing through.' Kirsten reached a hand up into the air and pretended to pull a bell. 'Choo choo!'

As Jessica cringed, glancing back down the path to see if anyone had heard, Kirsten pointed at two lines in the snow. They really did look like tracks of some sort. Not a train, though. The rails of a sleigh.

'Do you think that's Old Saint Nick out checking on us?' Kirsten said.

Jessica wanted to shake her head and tell Kirsten to stop being so Victorian, but on a certain level it was entertaining. 'You never know,' she said. 'Although it doesn't look like there were any reindeer. Those are boot prints. A person was pulling this.'

They headed on along the forest path which led around the side of the mountain, gradually angling up. Towering pine trees loomed all around them, but the path, lain with straw to stop them slipping, was illuminated by lines of fairy lights and regular lamps with little flames that may or may not have been real flickering inside their Narnian heads. Jessica leaned close to one, trying to see if it was real or fake, but from the warmth it was giving off, she surmised that it was real.

'They have a gas lighter,' Kirsten said. 'Mr. Dawes. He comes out at twilight every night and lights up all the lamps on the trails you're allowed to use. He said I could go with him one time. He said there's a trail that leads to a viewing spot right at the top of the mountain. He said on the Winter Solstice you can sometimes see the Northern Lights.'

Jessica smiled. 'This is Scotland, not Alaska.'

'But don't you feel the magic in the air?'

Jessica opened her mouth to let out a snarky reply, then closed it. Perhaps she ought to follow Kirsten's lead and allow herself to relax a little.

'I'm sorry,' she said. 'I'm trying. It's just that I'm worried about Grandpa, not to mention my flat, currently in the grip of a lodger from Hell.'

'That sounds troublesome.'

Jessica nodded. 'Yeah. It's a worry, that's for sure. Oh, is that it?'

She stopped. Just out of sight around the next bend, something was glittering through the trees. It towered above the surrounding forest, and as they came around the bend, both gasped with awe. Standing in a clearing was a huge, magnificent pine tree, brightly lit by strings of colourful fairy lights, decorated with bright red apples hanging on sliver strings. A huge star made out of wood, fir branches and holly berries was perched on its top. It was so big that it made the Christmas tree in the car park look like one from someone's living room.

'Wow.'

'Yeah. Look at that.'

'Such a shame they have to cut it down, isn't it?'

'Don't worry, it's got an infection,' came a voice from a bench nearby that they had been too transfixed with the tree to notice. Grandpa, sitting beside Charity from housekeeping, gave them a wave. His boots were covered in snow, and nearby stood a sleigh. Jessica baulked at the thought of her ninety-two-year-old grandfather dragging a sleigh up through the forest. Charity was plump rather than overweight, but her grandfather was stick thin, not even considering his advanced age. Jessica gave a stunned shake of her head. Perhaps she ought to start believing in Kirsten's magic.

'Scandinavian red pine beetle?' Kirsten said, nodding sagely, as Jessica snapped her head around. 'A shame. It's been ravaging through the fjords. Good to root it out before it spreads.'

'The very same,' Grandpa said. 'But don't tell anyone. The tree'll burn just the same.'

Jessica couldn't help but smile as Kirsten started off on a long, complicated exposition about the beetle's life cycle and mating habits. Since Kirsten was talking mostly to Grandpa, Jessica didn't feel rude as she left them to it and started up the sloping clearing, making a circle of the Yule Tree. It was easy to forget her troubles if she concentrated on the tree's brilliance. Staring up at the glittering lights while the chill air bit at her face, perhaps she was finally starting to feel Christmasy—

In her pocket, her phone vibrated. Jessica had forgotten she even had it with her, but guessed they must be far enough upslope to pick up a signal. Glancing back, she saw Grandpa, Charity and Kirsten pointing up at the tree, deep in conversation, so she unzipped her jacket, reached inside, and pulled out her phone.

To her surprise, there were two messages. The first was from her father. The first line was simply, *Getting on all right?* Jessica frowned. It was her father's familiar general greeting, which meant he had no idea where she was or what she was doing. It didn't matter; Jessica was used to it. She opened the rest of the message to read her parents' invariably more exciting news.

Departed this morning from Dover. The seas are a little choppy but it's all good. Your mother thought she saw a dolphin, but it turned out to be a piece of floating tarpaulin. I told her you won't see anything interesting in the North Sea! We've already turned up the coast towards Norway. Should start getting some good pics of the fjords in a few days. Will send you the best. See you in the New Year. And Merry Christmas!'

Jessica frowned. The last line felt tacked on like an afterthought. Typical of her father. No mention of her nor even of Grandpa now that her parents were occupied with their latest quest. Never mind. It was normal.

With some trepidation, she scrolled to the second message.

Doreen again. Jessica, who had been praying it might

be something as innocent as spam or a Christmas greeting from one of her clients, sighed.

I've had to call health and safety. Mick got stuck in the bath tonight. I've checked the contract and since you agreed to his stay he's technically a tenant. Don't you know he's on disability? You should have had safety bars installed. I'm afraid you're looking at a hefty fine, and really, it's all that you deserve. This place is a disgrace. Oh, and by the way, just in case something important showed up that you might want forwarded, I've been opening your mail. Nothing much of interest, just a few bills and a couple of bank statements. Although you did get something from a Snowflake Lodge. Is that where you are now? It looked pretty interesting, so Mick, Phil and I figured—

'Hey, Jessica.'

How many times would she need to ask before the ground finally swallowed her up when she needed it? Jessica, with the phone's screen inches from her face, swung around just as James Wilcox stepped out of the forest. He was wearing a woolen hat, and a thick mountaineering coatthat didn't seem quite right, as though the knitting machine had been off line. His cheeks were flushed as though he had been exercising, and she suddenly realised how Grandpa and Charity had made it to the clearing. From the size of James's shoulders, pulling the couple in the sleigh had probably been no harder than walking a dog.

'Oh, hello.' She hurried to put her phone back in her pocket, but it slipped out of her gloves and fell in the snow. She scrambled to pick it up, wiping snow off the screen.

'What are you doing out here?' His welcoming smile dropped. 'Ah, okay, I get it. Just up here because you can get a signal.'

Jessica felt her cheeks flush, but more than that, she was sick of being judged. 'Look,' she said, 'I don't know what your problem is with phones, but not everyone lives in the back end of nowhere, wearing sheep skins and dead minks—'

'It's from Marks and Spencer,' James said, touching his hat.

'I don't care. I'm sick of you looking at me like I'm some kind of phone addict. Do you have any idea what I'm dealing with—'

She took a step forward, but at that exact moment her left boot decided to betray her. She slipped on an icy patch of ground and toppled forward. The only thing she could do to stop herself crashing face down at James's feet was reach out for his coat. Her fingers closed over the edges of his front pocket as her left leg swung out behind her. For a few seconds they looked like a pair of amateur figure skaters practicing a routine, then James's pocket ripped and Jessica crashed down on to the snow.

'Are you all right? You have to be careful out here. The fresh snow tends to cover the icy patches underneath.'

Jessica's cheeks were burning. 'I guessed that.' She was still holding onto James's pocket, which had ripped off the front of his jacket. As her ears rang with embarrassment and shame, she handed it back. 'I'm so sorry. I didn't mean to.'

'It was an accident. It's fine,' he said, although his face showed something different.

Sorrow.

Despite her guilt, Jessica couldn't help but search for something to fill the awkward space. 'Perhaps it was time for a new one anyway,' she said, hoping James would smile. 'Have you written a letter to Father Christmas yet?'

James stared at the piece of material in his hand. 'My wife made this for me,' he said, giving a wistful smile. 'She never was the best with sewing, but she always tried.'

Jessica's heart lurched. 'Your wife … she's … um, not here anymore?'

James didn't look up. Downslope, Grandpa was shouting that it was time to leave, that the evening's hot chocolate extravaganza and magic show would be starting soon, that they needed to get a decent table.

'James?'

Still he didn't look up. 'She made this jacket for me on our third Christmas,' he said. 'Our last one together before she died.'

19

THE BET

THE MAGIC SHOW WAS FANTASTIC, WITH HOT CHOCOLATE and marshmallows appearing and disappearing all over the place, but Jessica felt in a terrible slump all the way through. Kirsten, sitting beside her, with Ben from the rental shop on the other side, clapped and laughed at everything as though she didn't have a care in the world. Jessica couldn't help but feel a little jealous.

After returning to the lodge on foot alongside Kirsten, while James pulled the sleigh carrying Grandpa and Charity from housekeeping, which included one exciting section where he climbed onto the front to steer as it slid down the steepest section of path, Jessica had been called off to attend to an urgent blocked toilet, and by the time she had returned, James was nowhere to be seen. Having avoided his eyes all the way back to the lodge, she had since gone over a hundred apologies but was yet to decide on the best one.

His wife had died. Whether she thought he was a little obnoxious or not, was beside the point. His heart had been broken, and she—unwittingly, but she couldn't absolve herself of all blame—had damaged a precious memory. If it wasn't that from the sound of things she had no home to go back to, she would have been tempted to jump straight onto the Tomahawk and head off down south.

After the magic show was over, the Silver Tours crew crowded their wheelchairs around the stage for what appeared to be a nightly karaoke session. As the first scratchy croons of Bing Crosby's *White Christmas* tore their way like an angry Krampus out of the speakers, Jessica headed for her room.

Kirsten had again been snacking, leaving her wrappers on the table in their kitchen unit. Jessica made herself a cup-a-soup out of a complimentary packet and used the microwave to heat a bread roll she had kept from breakfast. She didn't need to check the scales to know she was losing weight: her tummy felt tight and her jeans were hanging off her hips. It was Christmas; losing weight was unacceptable, and if she wasn't careful she'd be playing catch-up. She could only put it down to stress.

Feeling James's condescending gaze on her, she nevertheless opened up her phone messages to read the rest of Doreen's latest torment, only to find that the message had been clipped and she couldn't access the rest without heading once more to higher ground. What had Doreen opened from Snowflake Lodge? Jessica's pay slip? Her fingernails raked the tabletop with frustration, but there was nothing she could do from here. Enough was enough, though. In the morning, if she could find a working phone, she would call the letting agent and start proceedings to get Doreen out. It might take a demolition crew to do it, but if that was what it took….

Feeling the urge for company, she headed upstairs to the lobby. Left past reception, past a souvenir shop selling local food produce and locally made gifts, was a TV room.

Surrounded by comfortable armchairs and with complimentary sherry, hot chocolate, and mince pies on offer every night, a large cinema screen showed nightly Christmas movies. Today, much to Jessica's amusement, it was showing *Die Hard*. As Jessica settled into a seat near the back, she wondered if it was possible to hire John McClane to take out Doreen, or whether that was one mission too far.

The movie had only been on for a few minutes, when an old lady in a wheelchair rolled up next to Jessica's seat.

'Excuse me, dear, do you mind if I perch up here?'

Jessica smiled at the silver-haired lady who looked at least as old as Grandpa. 'Not at all. Isn't this movie a bit … noisy for you?'

The old woman's crinkled face smiled. 'Not at all. You'd hardly believe it now, but back in the sixties I was a stuntwoman for MGM.'

Jessica laughed at what was obviously a joke, but the old lady lifted a silver eyebrow.

'Don't believe me, do you, dear? I was one of the first. A pioneer. Had my career ended quickly when I lost my left leg from the knee down to a shark. On the set of one of the Bond movies, I think. I forget which one.'

Jessica was about to call her bluff when the old woman leaned forward and tapped an arthritic hand against her left shin. It made a hollow sound. Looking up at Jessica, the old woman smiled.

'Insurance paid a little better in those days. Got myself a cozy early retirement, and a little money for investments.'

Jessica wasn't sure what to say, so she just gave a dumb nod.

'Me and my sisters,'—the old woman hooked a gnarled thumb over her shoulder at two similarly old biddies sitting in their wheelchairs nearer to the screen, on which John

McClane was now jumping out of a building—'we found ourselves an old, rundown ski lodge, and decided to give it a brush up.' She spread her hands. 'It came out nice, didn't it?'

Jessica stared. 'You … you and your sisters…?'

The old woman grinned. 'My name's Theodora Bright. Over there are Trixie and Ellen. Born within fifteen minutes of each other, although my seven-minute head start makes me the oldest.'

'Theodora….?'

The name rang a bell from somewhere. Jessica frowned, trying to remember, but there was too much else to process for her to concentrate.

'You … and your sisters, you own this lodge?'

Theodora grinned. 'That hufty-tufty rushing about all over the place would have a fit if he knew we were here. I've already had him pick up a couple of things for me, just so I can get a better look at that toupee he's wearing under that bowler hat. Fancy that. He can't be more than fifty.'

'You three are the fabled conglomerate?'

'The very same. And we come here every year just to watch people enjoying themselves. You see, I'm ninety next birthday. I might not have many more. Gosh, Bruce Willis used to be a dish, didn't he? A shame old Father Time turned him into a potato. I suppose he turned me into a bag of old bones, so I can't go running my mouth.'

Jessica couldn't help but smile. 'Barry's always going on about you. Keeps saying you're going to close the place down or fire him, or both.'

'We'll do nothing of the sort while we're alive, and when we're dead … well, who knows what happens then? Don't tell him I said that, though. Keep him on his hoity-toity toes. Men struggle for motivation when they think no one's watching.'

Theodora started giggling, rocking back and forth in her chair. Jessica wondered for a moment whether the old woman was having a seizure. Then, gripping the arms of the chair, Theodora turned to her, eyes bright.

'By the way, I know who you are. Jessica Lemond, aren't you?'

'That's right.'

'Quite the run of luck that your grandfather's wife died and he was looking for one last blowout. We've always kept tabs on him and couldn't wait to offer him a position this year. Gives us a chance to settle an old bet.'

Jessica sat up. 'A bet?'

Theodora's eyes twinkled with excitement. 'I see nothing's changed with that old fool. He's still the charmer he always was. You can't help but love him, even though he left enough broken hearts in his wake to fill a Clinton Cards Valentine's Day singles bin. And although I might not look it now, back in my day, I was quite the looker. As was Trixie over there, my identical twin.'

'You're an identical twin?'

'Trixie and me. Not Ellen. A bit of a miracle, the doctors told mother, apparently, although the three of us have always looked pretty similar. It got us into some scrapes over the years, though. And a lot of fun, too.'

'I can imagine.'

'But there's one thing we've always wondered. And it's related to your grandfather.'

Jessica sat up in the chair, the movie all but forgotten. 'What's that?'

'Back in the fifties, before I moved into stunt work, I did a little acting. Not that much, but there was always a market for identical twins, and Trixie and me found ourselves with a bit part in a movie called *Double Trouble*, some terrible, long forgotten crime comedy. And your grandfather played the lead. Keeping in our role, we weren't allowed to have names on the set. We were Sister One and Sister Two, and the costume department kept us dressed the same, our hair the same, everything, all the time. But one night, your grandfather came over and asked me out on a date.'

Jessica laughed. 'Why does that not surprise me?'

'Well, we went out and had a little dinner and a dance and a pretty good time, if you know what I mean, but the next day, I heard from Trixie that he'd also asked her out on a date. We confronted him about it, and he claimed to have thought we were the same person. Unfortunately, production on the show wrapped not long after that and we went our separate ways. To this day, Trixie thinks he wanted to date her. And I think he wanted to date me. Which of us is right? This could be our last year to find out, and I wondered if you could help me.'

'You want me to find out?'

'Yes. I want you to ask your grandfather which Bright twin he was after, Trixie or Theodora.'

'Um, I don't know—'

Theodora put a hand on Jessica's arm. Beneath the leathery skin and the bony fingers was the remnant of a strength which might well have once hung from tightropes or jumped jet skis over sharks.

'If you do this for me, we'll reward you with a little Christmas present. Come on, make an old woman happy.'

Jessica laughed again. Everything was becoming a little surreal, yet fun at the same time. 'Sure,' she said. 'What present? I could do with a decent box of chocolates because I'm losing a little weight.'

'I can do better than that,' Theodora said. 'How about the lodge?'

20

SNOWBOARDING

JESSICA COULD BARELY SLEEP. EVEN THOUGH SHE COULD hear Kirsten snoring through the open door to the other room, she had far more on her mind.

After Theodora's shock offer, Trixie and Ellen had both wheeled over and confirmed what Theodora had said. Ellen, sounding frustrated, wanted the matter sorted 'once and for all.' Trixie and Theodora had then got into an argument before wheeling off to catch the tail end of karaoke, because 'that's when they start doing Cliff Richard.'

The lodge. The whole lodge. They wanted to give it to her, if she would only ask her grandfather which of two identical twins he had wanted to date.

It was like a crazy dream, yet when she thought about the nightmare her life in Bristol had become, it sounded increasingly appealing. Never having to go back there again. Leaving the letting agent to deal with Doreen and then selling up, moving to a ski lodge in Scotland where she wouldn't have a care in the world.

It sounded perfect.

Too perfect, perhaps, like she had fallen asleep on a comfortable sofa somewhere, her belly full of mince pies and hot chocolate, and was currently deep in the middle of a dream.

She couldn't be gifted with an entire ski lodge just for asking her grandfather a simple question, surely?

Dragging herself out of bed at seven a.m., groggily making coffee while Kirsten was still sleeping, she realised there was only one way to find out.

Leaving Kirsten to sleep, she headed up to the lobby, where breakfast was being served in the dining room. She looked for Grandpa, but he was again absent. Theodora, Trixie, and Ellen were sitting in their chairs around a table near one of the log fires, though. When Theodora caught Jessica's eye, the old woman lifted a finger to tap the side of her head while giving a secretive nod.

Just to check whether or not she was dreaming, Jessica went back to the lobby and out through the main doors.

A freezing wind was whipping across the car park, sending flurries of icy droplets battering against the windows. Jessica took one solid gust, then headed back inside, brushing herself off on the large mat just inside the doors.

If this was a dream then it certainly simulated cold rather well.

She headed upstairs to Grandpa's suite on the third floor. However, instead of having breakfast as she had expected to find him, his door was wide open and through it Jessica saw Charity from housekeeping piling sheets in the middle of the floor. Jessica had a sudden gut-wrenching thought that Grandpa had died in the night and no one had told her, but then Charity looked up and smiled.

'Are you after Mr. Lemond? I'm afraid he's already gone out. He's hitting the slopes this morning.'

It took a couple of seconds for Jessica to fully comprehend what Charity was saying. 'You mean he's gone *skiing?*'

Charity shook her head, and Jessica felt a momentary relief. 'No, not skiing. He says skiing is for old people.' Charity gave a quick chuckle that suggested she might actually quite like Grandpa. 'He's gone boarding.'

'Boarding … snowboarding? Are you serious?'

Charity shrugged. 'He's a funny old chap, and I enjoy hanging around him, but he's not a person to do as he's told. I gather his dead wife was a bit of a bossy boots?'

'Something like that. So he's gone up to the ski slope?'

Charity nodded. 'He said the powder's best first thing in the morning. After lunch it's too cut up to be much fun.'

Jessica didn't know whether to laugh or feel horrified, so she thanked Charity and turned to leave. Just as she reached the big window on the landing outside Grandpa's suite, her phone pinged.

She had forgotten that there was a small reception hotspot just outside Grandpa's suite. Guests weren't technically allowed on this floor unless they were staying in one of the three exclusive suites—the others were currently empty due to late cancellations—but Jessica had taken advantage of her staff status and family connection. Now, as she climbed back down the stairs and stepped past a STAFF ACCESS ONLY sign at the bottom, she pulled out her phone and scrolled through her messages.

Doreen's message had finally updated. Jessica opened it, certain things couldn't get worse than what she had already read.

But they could.

It looked pretty interesting so Mick, Phil and I figured we'd take advantage of these friends and family coupons you've been sent. It'll take a day or two to get organised—particularly considering that we've had to leave our stuff in the middle of the floor because I think you have mice living in one of the closets—but we'll be up there by the weekend. It'll be awesome to see you again, Lemons. In a way I've really missed you.

Jessica dropped the phone. It hit the carpet with a loud thump.

'My worst nightmare,' she said to the empty corridor. 'My worst nightmare is coming true.'

She downed a stiff good morning glass of sherry in the dining hall, then headed for the ski rental shop. If Grandpa could carve up the slopes at ninety-two, she could handle them at twenty-nine. And the sooner she asked him Theodora's immortal question and had the lodge signed over to her, the sooner she could put up some kind of professional blockade on Doreen staying. She didn't want to think about the chaos her lodger might cause.

Ben asked if she'd ever skied or boarded before. Jessica gave a confident shake of her head, because how hard could it be? All you had to do was point downhill and slide. Easy. With a knowing smile Ben lent her a staff snowboard, showed her how to strap it on, then offered her a couple of pieces of protective gear which she refused. He then politely suggested she might do well to sign up for a couple of lessons, but Jessica shook her head.

'I'm good,' she said, images of jumping off ramps and spinning three-sixties in her mind. 'No problem.'

The slopes were accessed by a set of stairs behind the lodge. For a couple of minutes Jessica trudged through enchanting forest, before emerging at the bottom of a clear ski slope which seemed worryingly steep. To her left was a small chair lift rising up the hill. Carrying her board over, she waved at the man inside the lift's operation room. Mr. Dawes opened a window and leaned out.

'On you get, lass.'

Jessica walked over to the lift. Two-person chairs hanging from a metal cable came zooming down the hill, into the lift station, where they briefly slowed, going around a corner and then accelerating up the hill again. Jessica waited for the lift to stop for her to get on, but as chair after chair rose past her, she became increasingly frustrated. Mr. Dawes was frowning at her through the kiosk window.

'Are you going to get on?' he shouted. 'Or are you just going to stand there?'

'I'm waiting for it to stop!'

Mr. Dawes laughed. 'It doesn't stop, lass. You stand by that line over there, then sit down as it comes up behind you. Never done this before, have you? Wouldn't it be an idea to get an instructor? One of ours is just up the hill now.'

'I don't need an instructor!' Jessica shouted, knowing that really, she did. But if Grandpa could do it….

Summoning all her courage, she stepped in front of the chair lift. It came up before her frighteningly fast, gave her bum a solid bump before scooping her up. She hung on to a side handle as the lift chair rushed up the hill, far higher off the ground than it looked from below. At first she hung on for dear life, trying not to scream. As she got used to the bumps of the chair and the way it jumped every time they went past a cable tower, she began to enjoy it a little more. The ski slope was off to her right, with the lift following a line through the trees before angling back across to the top of the slope. Below her, she saw mounds of powder snow, but also lines in it where skiers and boarders had gone off-piste, cutting through the trees. As she watched, someone came rushing down on a snowboard, hacking around a tall fir, jumping off what appeared to be a snow-covered rock, before racing away through the trees. She wondered who it was; she couldn't recognise the person beneath all the clothing, but they had appeared to be carrying a large hiking rucksack on their back. Jessica could only smile in awe at the snowboarder's skill.

As her chair reached the top lift station, Jessica was faced with the challenge of getting off the thing while it was still moving without falling face down in the snow. She braced herself as it slowed, then pushed off as solid ground appeared beneath her feet.

It looked as though she had made it as she took a couple of awkward steps forward, but then, as it started its arc around to head back downslope, the corner of the chair nudged her bum and she went tumbling forward. The snowboard fell out of her arms and slid gracefully into a snowdrift behind the lift station, but Jessica landed on her chest, arms and legs spread-eagled. From behind her came a groaning generator noise, and she looked behind her to see the lift wire had come to a halt, the nearest chairs rocking gently back and forth.

A door opened in the kiosk and a young man came running out. 'Are you all right?' he said, helping her up.

'I'm fine,' she muttered. 'I thought they didn't stop.'

The young man smiled. 'Only when someone falls off or when children are getting on. Do you need any help? Is this your first time on a ski slope?'

Jessica gave him a grim smile and marched off to retrieve her snowboard. Then, dragging it around the corner away from the lift, she sat down at the top of what appeared to be a sheer cliff made of packed snow. As her heart thundered in her chest, a couple of skiers got off the lift behind her, made a graceful turn, and then hared off downhill, quickly disappearing into the swirls of mist drifting across the slope.

Where was Grandpa?

Jessica sat quietly for a few minutes, contemplating her oncoming doom. Then, with her heart still thundering, she fixed on the snowboard as Ben had shown her, and tried to stand up.

She almost made it. Just as she was about to reach an upright position, her feet slid a couple of inches and she fell back down on her bum.

The snow was a lot harder than it looked. Three attempts later, she now understood why Ben had offered her a pair of padded trousers which in her vanity she had refused. Her bum was freezing cold, and every time she fell back down it felt like someone was whacking her with a frying pan.

The slopes were mercifully empty. She guessed that most of the Silver Tours lot were past winter sports now, but a couple of teenagers she had seen working about the lodge came past, gave her a wave, and then raced off down the slopes. With her efforts she had managed to make it about twenty metres downslope from the lift station, but she was cold and tired, and her thighs felt on fire from the way the board pulled at her legs.

'Ms. Lemond!'

Jessica looked up at the familiar voice. Off to her left, the lift chairs were passing overhead. Kirsten, looking wide awake and full of life with a snowboard strapped to her dangling left foot, gave her a wave. Beside her sat a young man Jessica didn't recognise.

'Gotta move,' she muttered, pushing herself gainfully up to her feet. This time she slid a couple of inches before the board jagged on a compressed lump of snow and pitched her face first downslope. She had just managed to awkwardly get her legs and the board back over to the front when Kirsten, gliding like a pro, skidded to a stop beside her.

'I didn't know you boarded,' Kirsten said, as her companion came up beside her. 'By the way, this is Clifford from the book club.'

Jessica gave a confused shake of her head. Book club? And for someone with such a dorky name, Clifford oozed utter cool. 'It's my first time,' she muttered.

'Did you see your grandfather? Isn't he awesome? He's been hitting up the tree lines to the right, but he'll probably swing past in a bit. He said he was going to do one last run before heading in to breakfast.'

Jessica wished her head would just explode and get things over with. 'Uh,' she said.

'Let's roll, Kirst,' Clifford from the book club said. 'You wanna hang the rails on the way down? I reckon I've got one more three-sixty in me. Then we'll head in and hit the buffet before getting on with those Tom Hardy critiques.'

'The actor?' Jessica mumbled.

'The writer,' Clifford said. 'Best turn of phrase in the nineteenth century. Isn't that right, Kirst?'

'Yee-hah,' Kirsten said, fist pumping the air. With a graceful jump, she swung her snowboard around, facing downslope. 'See you in a bit, Ms. Lemond,' she said, pushing off into a graceful slide.

'Nice to meet you, um, Ms. Lemon,' Clifford said, hurrying to catch up.

As they raced off into the mists, Jessica could only mumble, 'It's Lemond with a D!'

Kirsten's apparent mastery of a snowboard wasn't something Jessica wanted to think about. As she bum-shuffled her way downslope, she tried to concentrate on the hot chocolate that would be waiting and hopefully whatever was left over from the breakfast buffet. If she really shuffled hard, she might make it before the nine-thirty closing time, but her entire lower body was soaked on the outside and beginning to freeze on the inside. Her shoulders and back only felt warm from the sheer exertion of trying to push herself sideways down the ski hill.

She was about halfway down when she heard another boarder come to a sliding halt behind her. A shadow with two heads fell over her, and Jessica looked up to find James standing over her. Strapped like an oversized child to his back was Grandpa.

'We wondered who that total beginner was,' Grandpa laughed. 'There are instructors here for a reason, dear.'

'Are you all right down there?' James asked.

Jessica felt the wall of stubbornness she had carefully cultivated around her cracking like the icing on a chocolate log. She gave a desperate shake of her head.

'No,' she gasped, trying not to cry.

21

RAILWAY LINE

'THERE,' JAMES SAID, HANDING HER A STEAMING MUG OF hot chocolate. 'That should sort you out. It's a bit too early in the morning for a brandy top, but if you feel the need, just go and ask Trish in the kitchen. She'll hunt out a bottle for you.'

Jessica cupped her hands around the mug, feeling the warmth soaking into her freezing fingers. 'This will be fine,' she said. 'And, um, thanks for rescuing me.'

James smiled. 'No problem at all. I couldn't just leave you there. After I dropped your grandfather back at the lodge I thought I'd come back and check. You'd probably gone another twenty feet, but you still had a way to go.'

'I appreciate it.'

Jessica still remembered the way James's strong hands had felt on her shoulders as he helped her stand up on the board. Then, holding on to her, he had guided her down the slope to the ski lift. He had asked if she wanted to do another run, but Jessica had decided one was enough for the day.

'I gather you're not the kind of person who likes to be given any help,' James said. 'That's fine. Is that feminism?'

'I used to think it was. I think it's just called being stubborn.' She wondered if James had laced her hot chocolate with some brandy after all, because as she looked at his beaming face, cheeks flushed from the cold, fair hair curling out under the wooly hat he still wore, she felt the urge to tell him everything. 'The thing is, I grew up surrounded by entitlement. Thanks to Grandpa, my parents never needed to work, and I could have anything I wanted. Instead of turning into a brat like I suppose I could have done, it just made me jaded. By the time I was fifteen I didn't want anything that I hadn't earned myself. It's why I started my own business, got my own mortgage. It does make it hard to ask for help sometimes, though.'

'I'll tell you what. Give me an hour a day for the next three days to teach you the basics. After that, I think you'll be good to go. It's no harder than riding a bike, really.'

'Thanks. I appreciate it. So, eight-thirty tomorrow morning then?'

James frowned, and Jessica felt a sudden bloom of embarrassment, as though she'd mistaken his kindness for something more, and bullheadedly asked him out on a date.

'Actually, we'll start in two days,' he said. 'The first day is the worst, and I'm pretty sure you'll struggle to get out of bed tomorrow.'

The ache was already setting in around Jessica's shoulders and back. 'Thanks,' she said again, wanting to say something more, to ask him a question that had been burning the tip of her tongue, but losing her nerve. Instead, she said, 'I thought you did the reindeer sleigh rides. I didn't know you were a snowboarding instructor.'

James shrugged. 'In these parts you have to be a jack-of-all-trades to get by. I run the farm in the summer, but in the winter there's not a lot to do. I also teach skating and ice hockey up on the lake when it freezes over. We've not had a long enough cold spell yet this year, but probably by the end of the week the ice will be thick enough.' He smiled again. It was a nice smile, Jessica had to admit. 'Just think of me as the local odd-job man.'

Jessica was about to say something when the tinkle of a bell indicated a staff announcement through the speakers overhead.

'Jessica Lemond to reception,' came Barry's irate voice. 'There's a blocked toilet in Room 25. Hurry up, please. It's beginning to overflow.'

Cringing with embarrassment, Jessica stood up, trying to ignore the pull of her stiff hamstrings. 'I'd better go,' she said. 'It was nice talking to you. And thanks again.'

'Eight-thirty on Friday morning,' James said. 'If I don't see you before.'

It took her half an hour to unblock the toilet, someone having overindulged at the previous evening's buffet. By the time she had gone back to her room to shower and change, it was nearly lunchtime, but her arms were starting to tighten up. She was used to physical work but the sheer effort of trying to shuffle down a ski slope on a snowboard which refused to behave had used an entirely different set of muscles to the ones she used to unblock pipes. She could see herself getting up tomorrow morning and not being able to brush her teeth.

In an attempt to both avoid turning into a rusted up robot and keep her mind off Doreen's threatened arrival, she decided to take a walk outside. The snow had stopped and the air was clear and crisp, a light breeze biting at her cheeks. The faint tinkle of Christmas music came from a speaker hidden in the trees as she headed for the woodland trails, the fresh snow crunching under her boots. Where the trails separated a short distance into the woods, with one heading uphill to the hot spring and another down into the valley, she had seen the signpost for the lake before but never taken it. This time she followed the trail as it wove deeper into the woods, making a gradual angle uphill before cutting sharply back down. Then, to her surprise, it entered a short tunnel brightly lit with fairy lights, and Jessica realised the path had intersected with an old train line. It headed through the tunnel, the path wide, flat, and easy to follow. When she emerged on the other side, she found herself in a crystalline valley with snow-covered trees rising sharply all around her. A little further on, she came to an old train station building. Rather than fall into disrepair, however, it had been renovated and refitted, painted with subtle forest colors and lit up with Christmas lights.

Jessica climbed up onto the platform. The old train line continued on, following the line of the valley until it disappeared into the trees. The snow was hard-packed, but the lines of twin rails and the scuffle of feet were visible.

This had to be the track for the sleigh rides, she realised. She was about to climb down off the platform when a door opened behind her and someone stepped out of the old station building.

An old man wearing a Christmas hat.

'Hello, lassie, you're a long way from civilization,' said Mr. Dawes, the hat appearing comical on his stern old face. 'Didn't you see the no access sign on the other side of the tunnel?'

Jessica shook her head. 'I'm afraid not.'

'Ah, must have forgotten to put it up. I'll run back and do it in a bit.'

'Sorry, am I not supposed to be here?'

Mr. Dawes smiled. It reduced the natural anger of his face by about half. 'I'm just getting a few things ready,' he said. 'Since you're here, you might as well come and have a look.'

He waved her in through the door, and Jessica found herself in a room that, on the inside, resembled a log cabin. Through one door at the far end, in what had once been a waiting room, a series of machine tools were set up, and a number of wooden toys in various stages of completion sat on a line of worktops. Some were still being fitted together, others looked ready to be painted, more were sitting around waiting to have ribbons tied around them. Some were dolls, others were wooden vehicles, animals, little houses, clocks.

'I can see why I'm not supposed to be in here,' Jessica said. 'I feel like I'm intruding on Father Christmas's workshop.'

'Just me,' Mr. Dawes said. 'Every afternoon, when I'm done with my other duties. The last two weeks before Christmas we open up as a grotto. Most of the stuff is from local shops, but I like to make a few special things for the orphans.'

'Orphans?'

'There's a kids' home in Edinburgh which visits every year,' Mr. Dawes said. 'Those lads and lassies don't get the best start in life, so we help them out any way we can. Isn't that what Christmas is all about?'

Jessica nodded. 'It is,' she said, her problems and issues suddenly seeming so trivial.

'Get a little of the Christmas spirit into these kids, and

it helps them deal with their problems,' Mr. Dawes continued. 'And it shows that someone cares.'

Jessica wiped a tear away from her eye. 'That's lovely. If there's anything I can do to help…?'

Mr. Dawes grinned. 'Actually, I'm having real trouble with the hot water pipe in the kitchen we've got back there. It has a tendency to freeze up. Any chance you could take a look?'

'Sure,' Jessica said. 'Historical buildings are my specialty. I imagine this place is pretty old.'

'Built in the eighteen-nineties, closed in the nineteen-sixties, along with most of Britain's railways,' Mr. Dawes said. 'The government did a great job of cutting out the heart of Britain's rural communities, although a few of the old lines were saved for decent nature and historical trails.'

'How far does this line go?'

Mr. Dawes pointed through the trees. 'If you have a couple of hours free for a trudge in the snow with an old man, I'll show you. I need to go and put up that sign first. No one's supposed to be down this way until the lake opens for skating on Sunday. The ice isn't thick enough yet. And I haven't got around to stringing up the lights.'

'The lights?'

'Around the lake. To be honest, it's more of a pond than a lake, far too narrow for proper skating, and it's really cold, but we have a cabin down there with heaters and a kettle, and once I've got the lights up in the trees it looks proper festive.'

'I can help you if you like. I'm kind of on-call but my assistant Kirsten can fill in if I'm up here.'

Mr. Dawes smiled. 'Grand. Will keep old Humpty Trumpty off my back if you could.'

'Barry?'

'Yeah. The old fool's constantly terrified we're on the

verge of bankruptcy. Won't hire enough staff. Reckons this "conglomerate" is going to shut the lodge if it doesn't perform.'

Jessica smiled. 'I don't think they are.'

Mr. Dawes winked. 'Between you and me, I think he's a bag of hot air. But that kids' home I mentioned? Like me, he came from there. This lodge gave him a home, and later a job. If he loses it, he's a lost boy all over again. This place is his life.'

'I understand.'

'Don't tell him I told you. He wants everyone to think he's a big, bad manager, but he's not. Inside he's a frightened little boy, afraid of having nowhere to go.'

Jessica clenched a fist. 'Then let's get to work.'

Mr. Dawes grinned. 'Time for a hot chocolate first?'

Jessica shook her head. 'This time, no. Hot chocolate is for closers.'

Mr. Dawes laughed. 'Then let's close.'

22

STRINGING LIGHTS

THE PIPES IN THE OLD RAILWAY STATION TURNED OUT TO
be corroded. Jessica had to make a quick hike back to the
lodge to get her tools, where she informed Barry that she
was helping Mr. Dawes with some maintenance work, and
told him to call Kirsten if there were any emergencies at
the lodge. Kirsten, seemingly recovered from her thrills on
the ski slope, was up in the library, reading out of a big
hardback tome with symbols instead of letters on
the spine.

By the time Jessica got back to the grotto, she found
Mr. Dawes had made a plate of sandwiches. 'No work goes
well on an empty stomach,' he said. 'And we have coffee.
But like you say, no hot choc until the job is done.'

After finishing the sandwiches—mountain goose and
cranberry, so Mr. Dawes claimed, although it tasted a lot
like chicken to Jessica—they headed down to the lake
along a path that led through the trees across the tracks
from the old station. Jessica found Mr. Dawes was right: it
was more of a pond than a lake, perhaps thirty metres long
and ten across. Big enough for a little sliding around, but

certainly not large enough for any great theatrics. However, the setting was stunning. Behind them, the hill had sloped gently down through the trees, but the far side was set against a narrow bank, behind which a towering rock wall rose, all snow-covered crags and ledges. It felt like a secret place, one discovered by chance, a place where your thoughts could run free and the rest of the world was too far away to touch. Jessica sat down on a bench in front of the little cabin and stared up at the cliff, marveling at the small trees protruding from the rock, their leafless branches like gnarled hands catching bundles of snow.

'Ahem, no sitting down on the job,' Mr. Dawes said.

Jessica jumped up. 'Right you are. It's just … magical.'

'Isn't it just? It's on lodge land. You think those old biddies would sell up and risk losing this? Not a chance.'

'You know about them?'

Mr. Dawes chuckled. 'I think we all do except Barry. Keeps him on his toes. And behind all the trumpeting, he does a decent job.'

Around the side of the cabin was a storage shed. Mr. Dawes emerged with a wheelbarrow and several boxes of heavy-duty fairy lights. 'These run on solar power,' he said. 'They charge up during the morning and come on whenever they're out of the sun. The lake is at its best just after sundown when they're all glowing bright.' Then, with a grumpy harrumph, he added, 'It's yet another of my jobs to walk round this lake each morning and knock the snow off the power panels. No wonder I'm sixty but look eighty.'

'You don't look a day older than fifty-five.'

'Well, aren't you the charmer. Let's get hauling before my fingers freeze off.'

Jessica, insisting despite Mr. Dawes's protests, pushed the wheelbarrow, with the old man trudging along beside her, carrying a shovel to dig through any places the snow had drifted too deep. Starting from the cabin, they strung the lights through the low-hanging tree branches, tying the shoebox-sized solar panels to the trunks facing the direction of the morning sun.

'Three-hour window,' Mr. Dawes said. 'Looks pretty, but it's proper cold down here. This time of year, you get the morning sun, but once it's gone behind that cliff you're getting cold. Although, sun be blessed, we get a last peek of an evening, just before sunset. Spectacular, it is.'

'I can imagine.'

Mr. Dawes glanced at an old wristwatch which looked made out of wood. 'In about half an hour you'll see for yourself. After that it gets dark real quick, and these lights won't come on until the morrow, so we'd better scoot.'

While it had been easy enough to hang the lights through the trees, getting them up around the back wall of the lake was another matter. The bank was too narrow for the wheelbarrow, so Mr. Dawes went first, holding the end of the light string they were currently hanging, with Jessica feeding out the wire as he stepped carefully across snowy rocks that lined the lakeside, hooking the wire over juts in the cliff wall or over some of the little shrubs growing out of fissures. The string ran out about halfway across, so he climbed back over, then lifted the next box and handed it to Jessica.

'Your turn,' he said, breathing hard. 'Too much exertion for an old fifty-five-year old like me.'

'You don't look a day older than fifty,' Jessica said with a grin.

Mr. Dawes laughed. 'See, hanging around with a lovely young thing like you is making me young again. A shame the old bones aren't convinced.'

With Mr. Dawes guiding her, Jessica made her way out along the narrow riverbank to where the last string of lights had ended. Here, the riverbank was at its narrowest. The lake was covered with snow, but Jessica had no idea how thick the ice right behind her feet might be. The bank was only differentiated from the ice by lumps of snowy rock and small shrubs poking out of the ground. Jessica kicked a little holly bush, the snow falling away to reveal delightful clusters of red berries. With a smile, she strung the wire through the upper branches.

She had just reached the far end of the lake, where a little weir allowed water to trickle out from under the ice into a rocky, snowy stream, when the string of lights ran out. Mr. Dawes waved her back across, and together they returned to the cabin before finishing off the loop by stringing lights around the shorter side to the right. On a tree branch that extended out over the weir, Jessica looped the ends of two light strings together, and turned to Mr. Dawes.

'Finished. Do we have time for hot chocolate before sundown?'

The sun had appeared again from behind the cliff wall, but was dipping into the trees. Mr. Dawes, however, lifted a final string of lights and shook his head.

'We've got one more to do.'

'But we've done the loop, haven't we?'

'There's still the tree. You missed it, didn't you? When it's covered in snow it tends to blend into the background.'

'What tree?'

'The Christmas Tree.' He pointed into the centre of the lake. 'Right there.'

Jessica stared. He was right. She hadn't notice it before, but now that Mr. Dawes pointed it out, she saw there was a tiny island in the middle of the lake with a pine tree about two metres high sticking out. Its branches were laden with snow, but with a few of the lights they had strung behind now emitting a faint glimmer, it appeared out of the gloom like a snowy oasis.

'It's in a waterproof pot held in place by rocks,' Mr. Dawes said. 'But don't tell anyone. Do you want the honour of stringing these lights over it or shall I?'

'You mean, walk out on that ice? How thick is it?'

'Oh, plenty thick enough. Wouldn't handle twenty people, but you must be light as a feather. How many mince pies did you eat today?'

Jessica made a quick calculation. 'Three. Plus two hot chocolates and a piece of some Christmas cake.'

'That's nothing. Off you go. Let an old man sit down for five minutes. No wonder I'm feeling all of my fifty years.'

'You don't look a day older than—'

Mr. Dawes chuckled and put up a hand. 'Let's leave it at twenty-five,' he said. 'I can handle that.'

Carrying the lights, Jessica started out onto the ice. The snow covering was only a couple of inches thick, and if she didn't lift her boots it slid right off, leaving the slippery ice beneath.

She was halfway across when she caught her foot on a lump of protruding ice and stumbled. In a moment she was sitting on her bum, the hard ice quickly chilling through her trousers.

'Ouch! I bet that hurt!' Mr. Dawes cackled from the bench outside the cabin. 'Quick, five second rule! Get up before it gets in!'

Not quite sure what he was talking about, Jessica pushed herself up and brushed the snow off her clothes. Then, carrying the lights delicately in one arm with the other extended to balance herself, she half slid, half hobbled the rest of the way out to the tree.

'Good job,' Mr. Dawes called. 'Give it a shake first,

then string those lights and you've earned your hot choc for the day.'

Jessica reached in through the snow and gave the tree's trunk a little tug. The accumulated snow fell away to reveal a pretty little pine tree. Poking the solar receiver into the earth around its base, she wound the lights through its branches, ending with one big blue light right at the top.

Almost at the exact moment that she finished, the sun appeared through a break in the trees, hanging low to the distant horizon. Jessica was momentarily bathed in a spotlight of burnt orange light, then the sun began its dip beneath the distant hills. She stood watching, breathless, aware that this was one of the moments of her life that she would never forget, when the power of nature transcended all her real world problems, and reminded her of just how lucky she truly was to have the opportunity to experience something so wonderful.

And then, as the last rays of sun dropped below the horizon, all the lights blinked on.

From over by the cabin, Mr. Dawes began to clap and laugh at the same time. 'Fantastic,' he muttered. 'Just fantastic.'

Jessica looked around her. Some of the lights were already fading out, the solar panels only partially charged, but the magic Mr. Dawes had talked about had given her a brief glimpse of its true wonder. She had a vision of laughing children whizzing around on the ice, lit by the stars and the ring of fairy lights.

'Come on back, lass,' Mr. Dawes called. 'You've done a fine job.'

As Jessica hobbled back across the ice, only slipping a couple of times, Mr. Dawes opened the cabin door and switched on the light. Immediately the roof lit up with fairy lights he must have strung earlier, and inside Jessica saw the cabin was far larger than she had realised. A seating area had enough room for around twenty people, while a little door led off into a couple of other rooms. One sign said toilets. The other something she didn't recognise, so she asked Mr. Dawes.

'The Finnish sauna,' he said. 'It fits about ten, bum to bum. Except on Christmas Eve, when you have to sit on the floor.'

'Why?'

'Because that's when the visiting spirits come to take a sauna,' Mr. Dawes said. 'According to Finnish tradition. You wouldn't make them sit on the floor, would you? You have no idea how far they might have come.'

'That's wonderful.'

The old man laughed. 'We have some special seat covers we put out just for the occasion. Nothing like a glide on the ice and then a warm sauna, followed by a steaming mug of hot choc and a sleigh ride home. Lovely for the kids and the couples.'

'What about the Silver Tours lot?'

Mr. Dawes grimaced. 'Logistical problem to get them out on the ice,' he said. 'They go on the sleigh ride, but getting them on the ice … I don't know.'

Jessica was staring at a couple of pieces of old wood stacked in a corner. 'Leave it to me,' she said.

23

THIEF

JAMES WAS RIGHT. THE FOLLOWING MORNING, AFTER waking up early to begin work on the plan that had been buzzing in her head since the evening before, Jessica found she could barely get out of bed. After the morning's struggles on the ski slope and the afternoon spent stringing fairy lights around the skating lake, she could barely lift her arms above her head. Feeling groggy, as though she'd been on the sauce the night before rather than hitting the sack just before ten, she stumbled down to the dining hall to get some breakfast.

This morning's menu included Scandinavian Christmas waffles, and an Italian winter soufflé. Jessica, ravenous, devoured a huge plateful, even though the sheer effort of getting her fork up to her mouth had her breaking out with a sweat across her back. Upon arrival, she had quickly spotted Kirsten across the room, sitting with a group of bookish types, most in their mid-twenties. Jessica, on the cusp of thirty, not to mention technically being Kirsten's boss, had begun to feel old. She had looked around for another familiar face to sit with, but seeing no one, had taken a spot at a free table near one of the fires.

Only as she heard Kirsten's untethered laughter drifting across the room did Jessica realise how well her formerly shy trainee was settling in. It felt like Kirsten was an animal let out of a cage for the first time, smelling the flowers, seeing the snow. Aware that she was responsible, she felt both proud and jealous at the same time. When Kirsten and her friends got up and headed for the ski rental shop, Jessica felt a pang of regret. They looked like they were having so much fun.

Never far from her thoughts, she remembered the words of Theodora. All this could be hers if she could only get an answer out of Grandpa. The ski run, the lake, the hot spring, the beautiful grotto on the train line … it was like a fairytale land, and it could all be hers.

She looked around for Grandpa, but he was nowhere to be seen. No doubt he was already out on the slopes, or rock climbing, paragliding, or some other insane activity totally inappropriate for a man of his age.

Outside, the snow had begun to cascade. Mr. Dawes, giving her a brief wave, stumped past the window, a spade in each hand, heading for the trails. He had promised to show her the rest of the train line this morning, after she had finished mending the pipes in the lake station. First, though, she wanted to finish off what she was working on.

She was just clearing up her plates when Barry's voice came over the loudspeaker. 'All available staff to meeting room one-oh-nine. Five minutes please.'

She groaned, because Barry loved to call team meetings at the most frustrating times, usually for some trivial matter that could be cleared up with a memo on the staff notice-board behind the reception desk. The most recent assembly had been simply to remind the staff to kick the snow off their boots before entering through the main entrance, a notification which had taken less time to explain than it had for people to sit down. Putting away her plates, Jessica caught the eyes of the kitchen staff, most of whom were wondering whether the "available staff" tag applied to them.

When she arrived at the meeting room a couple of minutes later, Barry was standing beside a table at the front, a stern look on his face, his arms folded. He snapped at Jessica to put her Christmas hat on, which she dutifully did, wincing at the stiffness in her triceps as she pulled it over her head. She took a seat near the front. Within a minute, twenty or so people had filed in around her. Mildred sat down beside her, leaned across and whispered, 'What do you think old Trumpton wants to lecture us about now?', just as Barry lifted a bell and gave it an angry little shake.

'Order, please,' he snapped, his arms stretched by his side as though he was about to pogo up and down with anger. When the room had fallen quiet, he took something from a chair behind the table and put it down with a hard thump on the tabletop.

Jessica frowned. A box of chocolate bars. Or rather, an empty box.

Narrowing his eyes, Barry said, 'We have a thief among us.'

A collective gasp rose from the assembled group. A few people leaned across to speak to each other in hushed voices.

'This is from the shop stores,' Barry said. 'And it's not the only box that has been raided. Someone has been helping themselves to the stock without paying for it. I don't need to tell you that this is completely unacceptable, do I?'

'Did you check the security cameras?' someone shouted from the back.

Barry's face flushed, and he pulled the Christmas hat off his bowler hat to briefly wipe away the sweat beading on his forehead, before replacing the limp, soggy thing in its former position. 'I'm afraid the ones we have in place didn't show anything significant.'

'There's only the one,' Mildred called. 'And all it shows is the lobby. And it doesn't even work.'

'Perhaps it was Father Christmas,' someone else shouted, to grunts of laughter. 'Or his elves.'

'I don't appreciate you making light of this,' Barry said. 'I will not tolerate a thief. If anyone has any information, please come forward with it.' He looked across the assembled group, but when no one seemed about to stand up or raise their hand, he gave a tired shrug. 'That's all. You may all return to your work stations.'

Throughout the meeting, Jessica had sat quietly. As everyone filed out, she took a couple of steps closer to the front table to get a better look at the empty box of chocolate bars. It was a festive edition of Twix, and looked rather yummy. As she followed the others out, closing the door behind her, she remembered where she had seen the wrapper before.

It was the very same one Kirsten had been eating.

24

INVESTIGATION

Kirsten couldn't be the thief. It just wasn't possible. However, her absence at the meeting meant Jessica couldn't immediately gauge her reaction for signs of guilt. She could, however, poke around in their shared room to see if there was any other evidence.

Kirsten was still out on the slopes. Jessica didn't feel right about going through her friend's things, but the bin in their shared kitchen was enough. Poking through it, Jessica found five wrappers of the stolen chocolate bar.

With a little shake of her head, she set them on the kitchen counter to present to Kirsten as evidence later. She wanted to make sure, so she went upstairs to the shop and asked Aaron, the young guy behind the counter, if Kirsten came in a lot. With a wry smile, he shook his head. 'Once, maybe twice? She's always in the rental shop next door, though. Talking to Ben.'

Jessica thanked him and left. The evidence was mounting. Where would Kirsten have got the chocolate bars from if not the shop?

They had arrived at Snowflake Lodge as a pair, and if

Kirsten really was the thief, it would fall on both of them. Jessica knew she had to confront Kirsten, but she had to keep it quiet.

She paused in the lobby to grab another hot chocolate, adding a couple of marshmallows from a tray for luck. A little sign beside the tray mentioned that these were marshmallows made from natural ingredients and by hand, produced by a small company in the Lake District. Jessica gave a surprised nod, having had no idea marshmallows could come from a plant.

Her to-do list was stacking up. First up was confronting Kirsten. Then she had to help Mr. Dawes, while putting her secret plan into action. And then there was the question of Doreen. Was she really planning to show up?

So much to do, and her body was screaming at her to rest. A lie down might help, but with a sudden revelation, Jessica realised how she could kill two birds with one proverbial stone.

The hot spring was open to guests in the mornings until nine a.m., then from lunchtime to nine p.m., with the time in between reserved for cleaning, or for staff. Nothing would soothe her aching arms like a steaming hot bath, and it also happened to be a phone reception hotspot.

She borrowed a towel from the rental shop, pulled on her jacket and headed out. It was a crisp morning under clear skies, with the ten centimetres of fresh snow that had fallen overnight shining like a pristine white sheet. As she headed for the hot spring, through the trees she caught glimpses of the ski slope, a handful of skiers and boarders carving back and forth. Again, she wondered how she would feel if all this belonged to her.

Unable to shake an odd feeling that she didn't really want to put Theodora's question to Grandpa, she headed up the path to the hot spring. As she had hoped, it was empty. She undressed and left her clothes on a bench, wrapped a small hand towel around her upper body before climbing into the water, setting her phone down beside her so it could pick up any incoming messages.

The water began to do its work, easing the ache in her muscles. She leaned back, her eyes closed, feeling the relief only a hot bath in the middle of a wilderness could possibly bring. No doubt Kirsten would say something awkwardly profound about Mother Nature, but Jessica was just happy to experience the peace and tranquility of—

Her phone buzzed.

She picked it up, careful not to drop it into the water. With a sigh of relief she realised it was just her dad.

Hello love, hope things are swell. They are here! Ocean swell that is. Had some right rollers off the bow this morning as we headed for Norway. Fantastic stuff to watch from the bar with a cocktail in hand. We'll send you a postcard if we're not wrecked. Only joking. Having a lovely time. Wish you were here with us. Have a great Christmas. Dad x.

Jessica rolled her eyes. The usual kind of stuff. Dad was just checking in to alleviate himself of any guilt at being an uncaring parent. Perhaps a postcard would one day show up, perhaps not. Jessica never expected one, but on a couple of occasions her parents had surprised her, usually when they'd got delayed at an airport and had run out of downloaded TV dramas to watch on the iPad.

'Sounds fun,' she said to herself, putting her phone back down, not bothering to reply. She closed her eyes, leaned back, and—

Her phone buzzed again.

This time, her nightmares came true.

Hey Lemons, sorry to keep you waiting up there. Make sure they have a room for us, won't you? I forgot to book and I'm about out of charge. Me, Mick, and Phil are stuck at Edinburgh services. Blizzard came in. Lucky they have a hotel here, although I might put a small claim in with your lot for the cost. Nothing about adverse weather conditions on these coupons. That's what I call a joke. As is this weather. I hope it's not snowing where you are. Phil's sneezing all over, might be allergic to snow. By the way, there was a small fire at yours the last night we were there. Mick's certain he turned off the grill so you must have faulty wiring. I could get you blacklisted as a landlord for this, Lemons. You'd better make sure we have a good time at this lodge place or I'll be writing a letter to the council—

'Shut up!' Jessica shouted at the phone. 'Just shut up and leave me alone!'

She lifted the phone and shaped to throw it, stopping just in time. Instead, she held it above the water and shook it back and forth, growling with anger.

'And this is the only hot spring in Scotland that's entirely natural yet cool enough to actually bathe in. It's believed the hot water comes from a subterranean reservoir more than five miles below the surface.'

Jessica stared as James climbed into view, followed by a group of teenagers in school uniform. As they spread out into a line around the clearing's edge, the first couple noticed her, and a trickle of awkward laughter passed through the group. Jessica stared at James, whose mouth had fallen open in surprise. So stunned at this sudden intrusion, Jessica barely heard the plop as her phone fell into the water.

'So, what are you going to do? It's something of a pickle, isn't it?' Kirsten leaned over her coffee like a housewife advising a neighbour on a replacement garden fence.

Jessica shook her head. 'There's nothing I can do. My phone's sitting in a bag of dry rice at the moment, but I'm not too hopeful it'll ever work again. I asked Barry about the nearest phone shop, but he said I'd have to go over to Inverness. There's one in a village a few miles over but he said it only opens in the summer. And with heavy snow forecast from tomorrow, he doesn't think I'd be able to get back. They're already getting cancellations because the roads aren't cleared.'

'Oh, that's too bad.'

'Yes … and no.'

'Really?'

'I told you about my nightmare lodger, didn't I?'

'Doreen?'

'Well, she claims that she's on her way up here. Apparently her and her two crazy friends are stuck at Edinburgh services.'

'Oh, that's a shame, isn't it?'

Jessica shook her head. 'No, it's wonderful. Hopefully they'll be snowed in until February.'

'You don't mean that. Where's your Christmas spirit?' Kirsten gave a nervous laugh, then looked about to apologise. 'I didn't mean—'

'It's okay. It's just that one reason I came here was to escape from her.'

'Oh, I see. Wouldn't it be better to confront your problems? Perhaps neutral ground would make a difference. Shaking hands between the trenches and all that?'

As Kirsten spoiled her sage words with something odd, Jessica frowned.

'Talking of which, can I ask you something?'

'Sure. Go ahead.'

'This morning you missed a meeting that Barry called—'

'Ah, yes, I heard about that from Aaron in the shop.'

'Really?'

'Yes. Someone's been dipping their fingers into the supplies, I gather.'

Jessica nodded. 'So Barry said. And it was a particular type of chocolate bar—'

'Christmas edition Twix, wasn't it?'

'That's right, but—'

'I loved those. Ben bought me a whole box because I said I love the little elves on the wrapper. It was so sweet of him. Clifford looked pretty crisp when he found out, not that I'm in a love triangle or anything like that! Do you think—?'

'So, you've not been stealing them?'

Kirsten looked stunned. 'Me? You think it was me?' A single tear beaded in her eye and ran down her cheek. Jessica suddenly felt like the worst person in the world. 'Oh, dear....'

'No,' Jessica lied, 'I didn't think it was you. I just wondered if you'd perhaps picked those wrappers up somewhere—'

'I would have put them into the nearest litter bin!' Kirsten sobbed, her nose running now too. Jessica wished the lodge would just collapse on her head. 'I can't believe you think I'm the thief. It's only because Ben is sweet on me ... or at least I think he's sweet on me ... do you think he's sweet on me? Clifford is just a friend, but Ben, there are feelings there for sure, despite the age gap. I mean, he's a year or two younger, but by the time we were say, thirty and twenty-eight, it wouldn't matter too much, would it?'

Jessica wanted to claw out her own eyes and stuff her ears with socks. 'Can't we just forget about what I said?'

'You think I'm a thief,' Kirsten sobbed into a kitchen towel she had pulled from a rack behind her. 'How can I continue working for you when you think I'm a thief?'

'Come on, I found half a dozen wrappers lying around, and the kid in the shop said you'd never—'

'So you investigated me!' Kirsten wailed, briefly turning her face up to the ceiling and bawling like a child with a skinned knee. 'You asked … around!'

Jessica stood up. 'Look, I can't deal with this right now. I'm going for a walk.'

Leaving Kirsten sobbing behind her, Jessica went out, hurrying up the corridor until the sound of Kirsten's sobbing had faded into the distance. Only then did she pause long enough to give her forehead a light thump against the nearest wall.

This was turning into a nightmare. Everything she did seemed to fail. The bullying sledgehammer that was Doreen was moving inexorably closer with her football-loving war host at her shoulder; James, he with the nice smile and the powerful shoulders, thought she was a phone-obsessed maniac who liked to expose herself to schoolchildren, and now Kirsten was heartbroken at their breakdown of trust. Like the icing on a very large cake of emotional suffering, Barry would be fuming with her too, because she'd somehow mislaid her Christmas hat.

The day felt endless, but it was still barely lunchtime. The last thing Jessica felt like doing was eating anything, so instead of heading up to the dining hall, she followed the nearest set of stairs down into the basement.

It had surprised her to realise that the room she shared with Kirsten wasn't actually on the hotel's very bottom level, rather a purgatory level before the full-on flames, but the hotel was built into the side of a hill so there were various stepped levels going even further down. One staircase below was where all the stored inventory was kept, rooms full of stacked tables and chairs, fold-out beds, baby's cots, heaps of extra blankets, towels, and bed sheets.

The second level below was for junk that might or might not one day have a use: broken microwaves and cookers, old air-conditioner units, boxes of old pipes, damaged chairs, sofas with torn upholstery.

And on the final level, one with doors that actually led outside to a covered staff car park where her father's Tomahawk motorbike stood thankfully out of the snow, was the fuel storage.

Tanks of kerosene for the room heaters, piles of firewood for the stoves. And in case they got snowed in and ran out, stacks of old wood which looked leftover from various construction jobs.

It was cold down here. Jessica stuffed her hands into her pockets as she poked around, climbing over fallen heaps of firewood, looking for the exact thing she needed.

There, in a corner she found it, a big stack of long, thin logs yet to be cut into chunks. Jessica had taken a short carpentry course as part of her plumbing studies and had found herself just as adept to working with wood as she was with piping. All she needed to do was hunt out an electric saw from somewhere and she was good to go. Leaving her selected wood near the door, she began poking among the piles of junk, looking for what she needed.

After a few minutes of fruitless searching, she figured she would need to ask Mr. Dawes. Having hoped to surprise him, it was a little disappointing, but there was one last thicket of wood in a back corner which might be hiding the treasure.

As she pulled away a plywood board leaning against a pile of logs, her eyes widened in surprise. Behind it, the pile had been hollowed out into a little den, and there, inside, was a rolled up sleeping bag.

Beside it, an empty box of Christmas edition Twix.

25

THE END OF THE LINE

MR. DAWES LIFTED AN EYEBROW. 'SO, YOU GONNA LAY this thief a trap or just tell Humpty Trumpty and let him deal with it?'

'Whoever had been there definitely wasn't there anymore,' Jessica said. 'There was nothing personal in there, just that rolled sleeping bag and a few empty boxes.'

Feeling a little nervous but unable to hide her curiosity, Jessica had found a torch and taken a look inside the little den. She had found a couple of cartons of orange juice, an empty packet of bread rolls, and a stack of light reading. The mysterious squatter was a big fan of the Christmas fiction of Jenny Hale and Debbie Macomber.

Otherwise, however, there were no personal items, and a quick search of the surrounding area had revealed nothing, suggesting the squatter had moved on.

While it creeped Jessica out a little to know that someone had been or maybe still was hiding out in the lodge, she felt intrigued rather than afraid. The kind of person who read books like *A Christmas at Silver Falls* was unlikely to be dangerous. If anything, she felt a little worried for him or her. It was cold enough in the basements during the day, so nighttime had to be freezing.

'We'd better fish them out soon,' Mr. Dawes said. 'It's likely that we'll be snowed in pretty soon. Not much getting in or out once that happens, not unless you're into cross-country snow hikes.'

'How bad could it get?'

Mr. Dawes grinned. 'A metre, two metres, maybe. We're in a bit of a micro-climate here. Could be raining five miles over, but here we're two feet deep in snow. That's why we string the lights high, so you can still see them. Proper magical it is.'

'Doesn't it worry you?'

'Why would it? Most of our guests come in for the season. We get proper stocked up, and because all the heating is wood-fired, we're good to go as long as the pipes don't ice up. Nice and cozy it is. You'll love it.'

'I already do.'

'Nothing better than being cut off from the world with plenty of mince pies, hot wine, and good company. I hear you ruined your phone.'

Jessica grimaced. 'Who told you that?'

Mr. Dawes grinned. 'Can you keep a secret?'

'What?'

'Young James Wilcox. He's sweet on you, don't you know. Always brings you up in conversation out of the blue. Like, I'll be complaining some tree's come down on the line and the chainsaw won't start, and he's like, I bet that plumber girl can get it started. Like, he pretends he don't know your name. He's sweet on you, believe me.'

Jessica's cheeks were burning. 'He hates me. He thinks I'm addicted to my phone.'

'Ah, he's got a bone about those things. Best thing you

could have done was drop it in the bath. Perhaps shouldn't have jumped up out of the water in front of all those kids.'

'He told you about that?'

'Couldn't keep the grin off his face. Just trust me. I've been around a while. I know the way these things work.'

'His wife … she died, didn't she?'

Mr. Dawes sighed. 'She did indeed. Terrible thing. Five years back it was, I think, off top of me head. Poor lad was heartbroken. Time heals and all that, though. He's still young.'

'How…?'

'How'd she die?' Mr. Dawes sighed again. 'Car accident. Not her fault at all. She was sitting at a junction on one of those little roads out there, waiting to make her turn. Big heavy duty American pick-up comes plowing through. Doesn't even indicate, just turns right into her. She never had a chance.'

Jessica gasped. 'That's awful.'

'Killed her instantly. Turned out, the driver was some kind of hotshot property guy from London. He was on his phone making a deal about a patch of land when he made the turn. Should have got a couple of years for manslaughter but his firm hired some slick lawyers who got him off on diminished responsibility due to work stress. He was transferred overseas right after.' Mr. Dawes shook his head. 'So, you can understand why James might have a few issues both with phones and people in high places. I don't believe he owns a car, and even though he's had dozens of offers for his land over the years, he refuses to sell.'

Jessica couldn't bring herself to speak. She just sat quietly, running a hand up and down the length of wood she had brought out to the grotto.

'So, you gonna tell me what this is for then or what?'

Jessica looked up. 'I had an idea. I need to cut this in

half, hollow a groove in the middle, then add some straps. On the other side it needs to be carved into some kind of point and then oiled and waxed.'

Mr. Dawes frowned. 'Isn't it a bit big for an ice skate?'

Jessica smiled. 'Not at all. It's for a wheelchair.'

Mr. Dawes looked at her for a moment, a glimmer in his eyes. 'Girl, you're really something. Anyone ever told you that?'

'I'm just trying not to be entitled, when it would be very, very easy.'

'Well, you're doing a good job. I'm guessing you're after a couple of dozen of these, aren't you? I've got you covered. Out at the end station, we have a stack of wood not being used. And I have the tools. We'll need manpower if we're going to get this done in any reasonable timeframe, but that can be arranged.' He stood up. 'Right. Let's get on the wagon.'

'What wagon?'

Mr. Dawes smiled. 'The wagon of hard work. Follow me.'

They headed out from the grotto along the old train line. Still off limits to guests, Mr. Dawes had been working hard to keep the line relatively clear of snow, and it was only a few centimetres deep as they trudged through the forest until another station came into sight. The lights twinkling through the trees were all green and red, the bulbs shaped like leaves.

'Welcome to Victorian Christmas,' Mr. Dawes said, as they climbed up on to the platform.

Not for the first time in this wondrous place, Jessica found herself staring openmouthed. The station building had been transformed into a slate-grey Victorian townhouse, complete with smoke puffing out of a chimney. Through latticed windows she saw a quaint café set up around a wide hearth, an ornate Christmas tree in one corner surrounded by intricately wrapped presents. Not a space on the walls was left undecorated, everything with a historical, vintage air. As Mr. Dawes led her inside, Jessica could barely contain her excitement.

'We're going back in time,' Mr. Dawes said. 'A few of us used to joke that this one was modeled on the childhoods of those old bats in Barry's conglomerate, but I don't think even they're quite old enough.'

A rocking chair stood in one corner. 'All the staff dress up like Dickens's Christmas Carol,' Mr. Dawes continued. 'There's always a scrap over who gets to be Scrooge, because all he does is sit in that chair and grumble. I usually go shotgun on that, but my day off is coveted.'

'It's amazing.'

'Sells only Victorian-themed drinks and cakes,' Mr. Dawes said. 'Everything made onsite. Would you believe that Demelza from the kitchen used to run a Michelin three-star bakery in London? She actually sold it to move up here and run our dining room. The woman's out of her mind, but she said it's all about location. She loves a turn on the slopes, too.'

Jessica was still struggling to find words. She was just about to mumble something when movement caught her eye as something shifted underneath the Christmas tree. As she let out a surprised yelp, a fat ginger cat appeared, weaved between the presents and rubbed himself against Mr. Dawes's leg.

'Ah, Muffin. My cat. She has a heated box back there. Doesn't come out much until the spring thaw.'

Muffin approached Jessica, gave her a quick miaow,

then proceeded to claim her as territory with a solid nose press to the ankle.

'She's very friendly,' Mr. Dawes said, as Jessica leaned down to give Muffin a quick stroke. 'We dress her up with a bow tie when customers are here so she fits into the period piece.'

Muffin had seemingly tired of giving her attention, so with a final flick of her tail she disappeared back among the boxes.

'One more place to visit,' Mr. Dawes said. 'The station at the end.'

They went back outside and started their trudge along the line. Deep in the valley, with the forest gorge narrowing, the sun caught them only with occasional shafts of light down through the trees. On either side of the line, however, Mr. Dawes had hung strings of lights around young pine trees growing up beside the path.

'Planted these myself,' he said, giving one a tap as they paused to knock the accumulated snow free. With a tingle of bells hung around it, the snow cascaded down, revealing a pretty string of lights. 'Got to make it magical for the kids, see.'

Jessica could only imagine what it would feel like to be eight or nine years old and travelling along this line. The thrill would be unlike anything they'd ever experienced.

'And there it is,' Mr. Dawes said, as lights appeared through the trees a half mile further on. Jessica's legs were aching from the trudge through the snow, but she guessed it would be a lot easier when carried by a reindeer-drawn sleigh.

As the building came into view, Jessica gasped. It wasn't a station building like the others, but a log cabin set in a forested clearing that straddled the line. Like something out of a Christmas TV advert, it was strung all over with

Christmas lights, and the garden at the front was filled with snow-covered illuminations. A large snowman wearing a ring of fairy lights stood by a snow-topped garden gate.

'Built him myself this morning,' Mr. Dawes said. 'His name's John. John Snowman. You follow cricket?'

Jessica gave a regretful shake of my head. 'I'm afraid not.'

'Never mind. Shall we take a look inside?'

They headed up the garden path, snow crunching underfoot. Jessica marveled at the stillness of the forest around them, almost able to imagine she was no longer in Scotland at all, but somewhere far north like Lapland or Greenland. And when she opened the door to reveal a beautifully decorated café with a grotto area at one end, she was somewhat disappointed not to find Father Christmas sitting inside.

'He'll be here from middle of next week,' Mr. Dawes said. 'Got a special guest star for a few days.' Mr. Dawes grinned. 'Said it was the one thing he'd never done in his career, was Father Christmas.'

'Grandpa?'

'Right. Said kids have to sit on a chair, though. His knees won't take the weight anymore.'

'I can imagine.'

As she took off her boots by the entrance and stepped into the cabin, Jessica's mind began to drift. He might never have done it commercially, but it wouldn't be the first time Grandpa had been Father Christmas. He had shown up on her parents' doorstep every Christmas Eve until she was twelve to hand-deliver a special present. Usually something he had picked up on his travels, she had treasured the unique gifts far more than anything her parents had half-heartedly bought from the Toymaster or Argos down in Broadmead and had Reg or Molly wrap in paper almost as expensive as the presents. She had started to guess her red-and-white clad guest's real identity around the age of seven or eight, but it hadn't made it any less magical. As she looked around the grotto, at the huge easy chair Grandpa's tiny frame would somehow need to fill, she couldn't imagine a better choice.

'Is this the kind of thing you're after?' Mr. Dawes said, breaking Jessica out of her daydream. He was standing behind her, holding up two pieces of curved wood. 'Got a stack of it out the back. Was rebuilding the kitchen wall earlier in the year after we had a leak. Tons of it left over.'

Jessica smiled. 'Perfect,' she said.

26

QUESTIONS WITHOUT ANSWERS

By the time Jessica and Mr. Dawes had made it back to the lodge, it was already dark. The large Christmas tree in the car park and the lights strung up around the windows and doors made it look beautiful set against the starry night. Unsure how her body could take any more physical punishment, Jessica rubbed her arms as they came through the door. A hard hour with Mr. Dawes's power saw had left her shoulders numb. She wondered whether when she woke up in the morning, she would be able to get out of bed at all.

Mr. Dawes made his excuses and left her in the dining hall. A group of the Silver Tours gang was sitting around a long trestle table, and Jessica smiled at what she had planned. Nearby, Theodora was sitting with her sisters. She mouthed, 'Have you asked him yet?' but Jessica shook her head and carried on. Behind them, on a long table right in front of the buffet counter, some of the teenagers from the school party were tucking into heaped plates of roast beef, mashed potatoes, and a pumpkin and maple syrup pie that looked mouthwatering. A couple of kids noticed her and sniggered, but Jessica was riding a wave of confidence so she gave them a smile and carried on her circuit of the dining room, looking for someone to eat with.

There was no sign of Kirsten, but at a staff table in a corner she found Mildred sitting with Charity from housekeeping. They waved her to a free seat, and seeing no better option, Jessica gave them a thumbs-up. As soon as she had gotten a plate of food and sat down, however, Charity sidled closer.

'I know this might not be the right time,' she said, manicured eyebrows rising menacingly, 'but I wondered if your grandfather has mentioned me?'

Jessica shook her head. 'I'm afraid not. I haven't seen him all day.'

'He's gone on a snow-shoe trek,' Mildred said. 'Poor James got lumped into carrying him up the mountain.'

At the mention of James, Jessica felt herself blushing. 'He must be strong,' she said, the words feeling worryingly coquettish on her tongue. 'I mean, Grandpa might be ninety-two, but he must still be pretty heavy.'

Mildred patted her wrist, giving Jessica a knowing smile. 'Built to carry reindeers over streams, that one,' she said. 'He'll be fine.' Then, with a smirk, she added, 'Before we worry about any proposals you might have, dear, we need to deal with the present one.'

Jessica was sweating but Charity seemed oblivious. 'I mean, I feel weird asking this,' she said, 'but I think he might propose.'

As she said it, Mildred leaned close, the white bobble on the Christmas hat perched on top of her ornate hairpiece bouncing up and down. 'Charity found a ring.'

'What?' Jessica was relieved that the attention had shifted away from her, even if the thought of her grandfather remarrying again at ninety-two—and just three months after the death of his last, much younger wife in circumstances many still considered suspicious—filled her with a sense of horror which left her unable to eat.

'In his drawer. I mean, it looks like some kind of antique, but why else would he have it?'

Mildred turned to Jessica. 'Charity's job is to tidy up, of course.'

Charity leaned forward, the bob on her Christmas hat dangling dangerously close to Jessica's bowl of minestrone soup. 'I wasn't going through his drawers, if that's what you think.'

'I didn't—'

'There are some near the door where we keep the cleaning stuff. I found it in among the furniture polish, in this little old box.'

'He was hiding it where she would find it,' Mildred said.

Jessica just wanted the conversation to end so she could go back to her room and pull the pillow over her head.

'It was so obvious,' Charity said. 'But I mean … I can't.'

Mildred was shaking her head. 'It's just impossible.'

Jessica thought she had misheard. 'You mean, you're not interested in my grandfather? You do know he's extremely wealthy? For better or worse, his fortune has shaped my entire life.'

Charity gave a sad smile. 'I'm not a materialistic woman,' she said. 'My poor late Alfred was careful with his money and invested well. I really don't need to work. I only do it because Demelza cooks the best mince pies in Scotland.'

The two women looked at each other and gave a conspiratorial snigger. 'I'd marry him,' Mildred said. 'Absolutely. A shame he's not interested in me.'

Charity turned back to Jessica. 'I mean, what do I do? How do you say no to Ernest Lemond?'

'Um, you just say "no"?'

'But he's a TV great. Shouldn't I be flattered?'

'Well, I suppose.'

'And you know, he's proper old. If I turn him down, the shock might kill him.'

Jessica shook her head. 'If none of his recent adventures have done it, I think you're safe. I reckon he's good for a hundred and fifty at least.'

'But what if he does pop his clogs? The whole world will hate me.'

Mildred patted her on the arm. 'Perhaps we should wait for Jessica to find out.'

'What?'

Mildred leaned forward. 'You can do it, can't you, dear? Just ask him if he likes her, what he's planning to do. Just so poor Charity here can prepare herself.'

'He's only due to stay until January, so perhaps I can avoid him until then,' Charity said.

Jessica couldn't help but chuckle. It all seemed so ridiculous, but she had never seen the two women so serious. She caught Theodora's raised eyebrow across the room and flashed the old woman a smile. Grandpa clearly had quite an effect on women, even at his advanced age.

'I'll see what I can do,' she said, quickly finishing off her dinner. 'Sorry, but I have to go and fix a blocked sink on the second floor.'

Tired of so much demanding company, Jessica headed back to her room. She found herself looking forward to seeing Kirsten. She wanted to apologise again for accusing her of stealing, and to let her know about what she had found in the storeroom. Kirsten, for all her eccentricities, was a lot more calming than the other people around her.

The moment she opened the door, though, she knew something was wrong. All of Kirsten's things were gone and a Christmas card stood on the kitchen table. Jessica scooped it up. The picture showed a forlorn little robin sitting on a snowy holly branch.

'*Dear Ms. Lemond,*' Jessica read. '*I'm sorry if I disappointed you. It wasn't my intention at all, but I guess if you think I'm a thief, then in your heart I'll always be one. I've gone away. I won't be back. I thank you for all your kindness over the last few months and for giving me the wonderful opportunity to come with you to Scotland. The motorcycle was quite the thrill, wasn't it? I'll settle for a slower ride home. Don't worry about me. I'm not large enough to be a satisfactory meal for a mountain lion. See you again, Kirsten.*'

Jessica groaned. 'You've got to be joking,' she muttered aloud. So, Kirsten had run off somewhere. The message contained all the usual awkwardness that Jessica was beginning to find charming.

She put the card into her pocket and headed back upstairs to the lobby. Mildred had returned to her spot on the reception desk.

'Have you seen Kirsten?' Jessica asked.

'No, dear, not since this morning.'

'I think she might have run off somewhere.'

Even as she said it, Jessica hoped otherwise. Through the windows, snow was pelting down, a vicious wind piling it into corners of the car park, leaving several vehicles entirely buried. Mr. Dawes had told her that for all the area's charm, when it decided to really snow, there was nothing to be done but drink hot chocolate, sing karaoke, and ride it out.

She wandered through the lobby area, looking for other members of staff. When she saw Barry talking on a phone, he lifted a hand and refused to look at her, snapping that he was busy with the 'uncooperative snowplow people'.

In the rental shop near the side door, she found Ben, just closing up the shop for the night.

'Ben, have you seen Kirsten?'

At the mention of Kirsten's name, he looked away. 'She broke up with me,' he said.

Jessica stared. 'What? You were a couple? How long?'

Ben sighed. 'Since yesterday. I thought she liked me.'

'What happened?'

'She showed up this afternoon and told me I was wrong about her, that she was nothing like I imagined. I thought she was a mouse but she was really a lion.'

'She actually said that? Sounds like Kirsten all right.'

Ben sniffed. 'She said I was better off without her. I thought she'd chosen Clifford over me, but when I saw him in the dining hall he told me she'd already been to see him. She'd said that while she appreciated his advances, they'd only ever be friends.'

'Well, that's nice and everything, but do you know where she went?'

'She said she was leaving.'

Jessica nodded at the snow pattering against the window. 'And how was she planning to do that?'

Ben shrugged. 'She told me not to worry, that she was a practical girl.'

'Changing a toilet U-bend is a little easier than escaping from a snowed-in ski lodge,' Jessica said.

Ben was giving her a strange look. Jessica wondered if he was going to say something profound, but then his mouth wrinkled and he started to cry. 'I loved her,' he said, opening his arms for Jessica to pull him into a hug.

'Don't worry, it'll be fine,' she said, patting him on the back, wondering if this was what it felt like to be the mother of an emotionally charged teenager. Who could have known Kirsten would be such a heartbreaker?

The side door opened and Mr. Dawes, caked in snow from head to foot, stepped inside, the wind whistling around his shoulders. Snow blew in around him, and he squeezed the door shut, then pulled off his jacket and shook snow out on to the big mat in front of the door.

'Blizzard come in,' he muttered. 'Brutal out there. What happened to the boy?'

Jessica smiled. 'He's heartbroken.' Then, to Ben, she said, 'Don't worry, plenty more fish, isn't that right?'

'Shooting fish in a barrel once the mistletoe comes out,' Mr. Dawes added with a gruff laugh. 'Handsome lad like you. If I'd had half your looks in my youth I'd have spent half my life in the—'

'Kirsten's missing,' Jessica interrupted. 'I found a goodbye note in our room. You don't think she's gone outside in this, do you?'

'Sensible girl like that, no chance.'

Outside, the lights strung through the bushes were slowly getting buried. The tree in the middle of the car park still glowed, but its lights were obscured by accumulated snow. Jessica couldn't help but smile. It was all very Narnia, very *Box of Delights*, very … Dickensian.

'She has, I know it,' she said. 'This would be exactly her thing, to be some Victorian heroine struggling through the snow. The problem is, the only thing she knows about blizzards is what she's read in her books. She'll freeze to death out there.'

Mr. Dawes gave a grim nod. 'We'll need a search party. I just came back along the main trail and didn't see her, nor no tracks. Let's go see what we can find. Lad, ready to be a hero?'

Ben wiped his eyes and nodded. 'I'll do anything for her.'

'That's good, because if she's sheltered in a mountain lion's cave we'll need someone to go in.' At Ben's startled expression, Mr. Dawes cackled. 'Don't worry, lad. Ain't none of them nested this close to the road.'

'Huh....'

'I think he's joking, Ben. Follow us.'

They headed for reception. Barry was off the phone, but was running backwards and forwards in front of a bemused Mildred, flapping his hands, his Christmas hat and the bowler beneath bobbing up and down like a concertina with his toupee, which had come unstuck.

'Tomorrow afternoon,' he muttered. 'What good is that? We have guests due in the morning. How are we going to get them safely up to the hotel? It's all falling apart. The conglomerate will go into a frenzy—'

'Kirsten's disappeared,' Jessica said. 'I think she might have run off somewhere.'

Barry stopped. 'What?'

Jessica grimaced. 'Well, you know that thief that you were talking about … I thought it was her. I found some chocolate bar wrappers in our room.'

'I gave them to her!' Ben wailed, so dramatically that it made Jessica jump. She was beginning to understand the attraction between Kirsten and the unassuming kid who worked in the rental shop. 'If I'd known it would cause so much trouble I would have bought her some crisps or something.'

'Did you pay for them?' Barry snapped.

'Of course I did.'

'Then who—'

Jessica put up a hand. 'We'll worry about that later. My friend is out in the snow.'

Mr. Dawes turned to Barry. 'Is James Wilcox here tonight? Only way we're getting through this is on a sled.'

'He went out with Mr. Lemond,' Barry said. 'They were planning to hike up to the peak.'

'In this?' Mr. Dawes said. 'Madness.'

'My grandfather's middle name,' Jessica said.

Barry, not understanding the joke, frowned and shook his head. 'But it says Cyril on his health insurance form—'

Mildred patted his arm. 'Relax, she was just—'

The front door swung open, and a snow-covered figure stepped inside. James pulled back his hood, showering the mat with snow.

'Wow, shows how the weather can change,' he gasped, cheeks red and chapped, his breath rising in a cloud of steam. 'We'd barely made it halfway up when the snow came in.'

He stamped his snowshoes and patted down his jacket. Some lumps of snow landed on the carpet just inside the lobby, and Barry shook his head.

'How many times have I said … where's Mr. Lemond?'

'Here!' came Grandpa's cheerful shout from behind James's shoulder. Grandpa's head appeared, covered by a wide jacket hood, a Christmas hat pulled down to just above his eyes. James pulled straps off his shoulders and lowered what appeared to be a giant child carrier to the ground. Mildred came out from reception to help Grandpa up into a chair, leaving a snowy trail on the carpet from Grandpa's ski wear. Barry, eyes wide, was literally turning in circles like a drill about to break ground.

'Brutal out there now,' James said. 'I need to get back to the farm, but I'll have to wait until morning.' He glanced up, saw Jessica and gave her a regretful smile. 'I'm afraid I'll have to cancel our lesson tomorrow.'

Inside Jessica felt crestfallen, but she tried to hide her

disappointment with a smile. 'It's all right,' she said. 'I'm still aching from yesterday as it is. By the way, you didn't see Kirsten on your way in, did you? She's gone missing.'

James started to shake his head, but Grandpa lifted a hand. 'We saw those tracks, didn't we? You thought it might have been a fox or something but they were too buried to tell.'

James nodded. 'Heading down towards the main road. Not like a fox to go that way, but we did wonder. You say Kirsten's out in the snow?'

'Yes. We had a … ah … a disagreement.'

'She'll die!' Ben cried.

Mr. Dawes told him to hush. 'If she's got a jacket on the lass'll be fine. Down towards the main road, you said?'

'Straight down the drive.'

Mr. Dawes nodded. 'Said she's a practical girl, didn't you?' he said, turning to Jessica. 'You know what's down that way, don't you?'

Jessica shook her head. 'What?'

Mr. Dawes grimaced as though about to reveal some deep, dark secret that only locals could possibly know. With one squinting eye and half his mouth turned up in an expression that suggested both fear and disgust, he spoke.

'*The bus stop.*'

27

RESCUE

G<small>RANDPA WANTED TO COME, BUT BETWEEN</small> M<small>ILDRED</small>, Barry and Jessica, they managed to dissuade him. Both James and Mr. Dawes thought it couldn't hurt, while Ben was still enamoured with predicted grief. In the end, with Mr. Dawes too tired and Ben too distraught to be of much help, a rescue operation fell to James and Jessica. With jackets, hats, gloves, and snow boots on, they headed out into the snow.

Up near the lodge the wind would have taken away anything they wanted to say, but they had only gone a few steps before Jessica began to feel the build-up of tension between them. James said nothing, walking a couple of steps in front, occasionally turning back to check she was following. The snow was knee deep in places, although the wind had blown it into thick drifts around the car park's edge. Jessica couldn't help but let out a cry of excitement as she stepped off a flowerbed and found herself up to the waist in soft, powdery snow. James looked back, his smile the only thing visible under his hood, then reached out a hand to help her out. Even through gloves, Jessica felt a thrilling tingle at their touch.

Once they were through the car park and onto the main driveway, the trees blocked most of the wind. The snow was a little shallower here and they walked side by side, following depressions in the snow that might have been footprints made a couple of hours before.

'I imagine this wasn't what you had planned for your evening,' Jessica said at last, finally breaking the awkward silence as they followed the lights strung in the trees alongside the drive, the lodge receding behind them.

James looked up and smiled. 'All in a day's work,' he said. 'I was planning to go back to the farm tonight, but the reindeer will be fine. They're all in the shed, and it's got proper bolts on it this time.'

'That's a relief.'

'I apologise if we scared you the other day.'

The first day they had met felt like forever ago. Jessica laughed. 'We must have looked like such city kids.'

'Well, kind of. Life up here takes a bit of getting used to.'

'I imagine.'

'No shops for miles, no phone reception.'

Jessica grimaced. 'I … I heard about your wife.'

James closed his eyes for a moment. 'Mr. Dawes told you?'

'Yes.'

'There's a surprise. He's always looking out for me. Acts like my grouchy old uncle. He thinks I can't take care of myself.'

'I think you can.'

James smiled. 'Takes one to know one. You know, we're not so different. We're both trying to prove something, aren't we?'

'I'm trying to prove I'm not like my parents, and you're trying to prove you're … not….'

'Not like the man who killed my wife.' James shrugged. 'I don't hate phones, I just don't like them.'

'I've barely thought about mine since I dropped it into the hot spring.'

'That must have been frustrating.'

'I'm not addicted to it, you know. It might come across that way sometimes, and it might sound like a cliché, but I need my phone. It's how I contact my customers, how I keep in touch with my family, and it's how I find out whether I'll still have a house to go back to when I leave the lodge.'

'I wasn't trying to be judgmental.'

'I can understand your feelings. I hope you can understand mine.'

They walked on in silence for a couple of minutes, and Jessica wondered if she'd been a little too forthright. She was tired of it, that was all. Tired of people getting the wrong impression.

'Well, we're here,' James said, as a single light up ahead illuminated a little wooden shed beside the snow-covered arc of the main road. They went inside, glad to be out of the snow still falling heavily around them. The wind had died down, but the snow was too heavy to see more than fifty feet ahead of them.

'She's not here,' Jessica said, then tapped a sign on the wall, which announced that all buses would be cancelled in the event of heavy snow. 'Now we have a real problem.'

'She was here a while, though,' James said. 'She sheltered for a bit.'

'How do you know?'

James pointed. 'Because those tracks leading up the road are a lot more prominent than the ones we followed down here. The snow hasn't had as long to cover them up.'

'Why would she have gone that way and not back to the lodge?'

'She's a stubborn one, I think. The nearest village is that way, although it's a hilly five-mile walk in the best of conditions. She must be out of her mind to attempt it in this weather.'

'She's a city girl. She's also a bit of a fantasist.'

'We'd better get after her before she freezes to death. Are you okay? If you'd rather go back, I can go on alone. I imagine I'm a lot more used to these conditions than you.'

While the thought of a hot chocolate laced with brandy and a plate of mince pies was extremely appealing, Jessica shook her head. Despite the circumstances, she was quite enjoying their time together. 'Actually, once you get used to the cold, it's kind of fun.'

James laughed. 'There's a bit of country in you, then,' he said.

'It must be my grandfather's adventurous spirit.'

James laughed again. 'You couldn't go wrong with that. I don't know where that old man gets his energy. He's an inspiration to us all. Even if I do have to carry him about.'

'You must be quite … strong.'

'It's good exercise.' James looked at her, and Jessica felt a blush coming on, so she looked quickly away.

'Come on, we'd better get after Kirsten before the tracks fill in.'

They headed back out. The rage of the blizzard had passed, with the moon beginning to appear through the clouds as the snow fell lighter than before. Behind the crunch of their boots through the fresh snow was a light pitter-patter of the settling flakes. Occasional streetlights illuminated sections of the road, giving them pools of light to aim for as they trudged up a gentle slope, trees to their right with moorland on their left beyond a low stone wall.

'Are you hungry?' James asked as they crested the hill and saw the road dipping away ahead of them until it was lost in the snowy gloom. 'I bagged a handful of mince pies before we headed back out.'

They found a sheltered spot underneath an overhang of trees where the road widened into a passing lay-by. James pulled off his gloves and handed Jessica a mince pie wrapped in foil.

'It's warm,' she said.

'Ah, that's because of the flask,' he said, pulling out a little flask and holding it up. 'Hot chocolate. Don't worry, it's not laced, just in case I have to drive the sleigh later.'

Jessica, unsure if he was making a joke or not, gave a nervous laugh. 'You're well prepared,' she said.

'Your grandfather and me were going to have a moonlit picnic on the mountain top,' he said. 'Unfortunately the snow closed in before we could make it. I think tomorrow night might be better. As long as you keep an eye on the weather, it's worth taking the risk. You can see for miles. You can see the lights of all the local towns. You should come.'

Jessica gave a nod that she immediately worried would make her look too keen. Luckily, James didn't seem to notice in the dark. 'Sure,' she said, trying to sound less excited at the prospect than she felt. 'Sounds fun.'

'Sorry again about cancelling our snowboarding lesson tomorrow,' he said. 'It's just that if I can't get back to the farm tonight I really need to head over in the morning, just to check on the reindeer. Make sure they've got food and everything.'

'It's okay.'

There was a pause. Then James said, 'If you're not

busy, you could come and help me if you like. Everyone thinks I'm this terrible loner, but I don't mind a bit of company.'

If Jessica had doubted whether or not she was attracted to James, her body was telling her she most certainly was. Her heart had begun to thump so loud she was sure he could hear, and she had a lump in her throat the size of an apple.

'Uh … okay,' she muttered.

'I mean, if you're busy or you don't want to—'

'I do,' Jessica blurted. 'I mean, it sounds nice. I'd like to come.'

'Great. It's a … uh, cool. I'll look for you in the morning.'

'Sure.'

'We'd better—'

'Yeah.'

They quickly finished off their mince pies and hot chocolate, then got back on the trail. Kirsten's footsteps were still visible, although in places they paused where she had sheltered for a while from the snow. With the pauses coming more frequently, Jessica felt certain they were getting close. She just hoped they found her safe and unharmed. While the temperature was only a couple of degrees below zero, she had no idea how well Kirsten was dressed. She wouldn't put it past her overly dramatic friend to have rushed off in her pajamas.

They had just reached a little junction with a road heading out across the moor when James stopped. 'Can you hear that?' he said.

'What?'

'It sounds like music.'

'I can't hear anything.'

'Listen carefully.'

They both stood in silence for a few seconds. At first all Jessica could hear was the gentle patter of the snow, but then she picked something up behind it.

'You're right,' she said.

'It's coming from up ahead.'

They walked on past the junction, following the angle of the main road as it arced around the hillside, heading gently uphill. As it straightened out again, they saw a light through the snow up ahead, and another sound joined the music, which was coming louder than before: the hum of an idling engine.

'It's a car,' James said. 'That's a little viewing spot up there. It has good views of the river valley. Someone's in that car.'

It took Jessica a moment to realise why the music sounded off. Then she realised.

'Someone's singing,' she said.

'More than one person,' James added. 'Sounds like a proper little party.'

The car was rocking from side to side as three voices rose in discordant unison to holler the lyrics to Wham's *Last Christmas.* Jessica cringed. She'd heard better coming from the Silver Tours group's nightly sessions.

As they reached the snow-covered car park, Jessica saw three sets of tracks. The one they had followed, with two others coming from the opposite direction. The way the snow was disturbed around the car suggested it had taken some time for these arrivals to get inside, but as Jessica came close enough to make out shapes behind the foggy windows, she wondered if her worst fears were about to come true.

'Well, looks like we might have found her,' James said. 'Do we really want to break up the party?'

Jessica took a deep breath. 'We'd better make sure,' she said, then tapped on the nearest window.

The singing immediately stopped as the rear window began to wind down. 'We're sorry, officer!' someone shouted in a Bristolian accent. 'We'll pay for any damage. We just needed somewhere to shelter for a bit.'

'Mick?'

The overlarge frame of Doreen's best friend took up the entire back seat. He was dressed in just a duffel coat with an Arsenal hat pulled down over his head. Jessica leaned in to see who was sitting in the front seats, but to her relief, neither appeared to be Doreen. One was most definitely Kirsten, a guilty grin on her face as she appeared tiny wrapped in two ski jackets. The other was someone Jessica had only seen briefly at a distance, but was dressed similarly inappropriately to Mick, in a Burberry jacket over an Arsenal shirt with an Arsenal beanie hat pulled down to his eye line.

'Are you Phil?'

'All right?'

Jessica took this to mean yes. 'Where's Doreen?'

Mick glanced at Phil, then lifted a can of Carlsberg and grinned. 'Bit of a story, that. Left the car at Edinburgh services due to the snow, but Dor found a bus heading out this way. Dropped us off in some village back there, driver said the snow was too much to go no further. We got a few pints in, but Dor picked a fight with some Celtic fans so we legged it.'

Jessica gave a slow shake of her head. 'Doreen started a fight?'

'Celtic have the Gunners in the Europa League next week,' Phil said, by way of explanation. 'They started mouthing off, so Dor heaved her pint over one, then got stuck in.'

James glanced at Jessica, one eyebrow raised. 'This is Doreen, your lodger?'

'The very same.' Jessica turned back to Mick and Phil. 'So you left her behind? I'm not sad, by the way. Just wondering.'

'Landlord called the pigs, so we bought a pack of tinnies and legged it.'

Jessica wondered at how realistic a timeline allowed for them to pause and purchase a pack of Carlsberg before running away into the night, but no doubt their story had distorted somehow from true events. Still, the absence of Doreen was definitely a sign that God existed, and perhaps even liked her just a little bit.

'And you ended up in this car?'

Phil grimaced. 'Sign said five miles, but you know, Mick's a big lad, and there's a bit of snow around. We'll pay for the damage, honest.'

'Whose car is this?' Jessica asked, although even as she said it, she thought she might know the answer. There had been something familiar about it from the moment it first came into sight.

'No idea,' Phil said. 'Had to pick the lock and give it a quick hotwire. I ain't no crim, though. Me big brother taught me. He did a couple of months once but he's straight now. Works in Carphone Warehouse.'

Jessica looked at Kirsten. 'And you just came across these guys out here?'

Kirsten smiled. 'The car was like an oasis in a snowy desert,' she said, then abruptly frowned. 'I'm sorry I ran off.'

Jessica returned her smile. 'And I'm sorry I thought you were a thief.'

Phil looked from one to the other. 'Looks like you two

have some issues you need to thrash out over a few pints,' he said.

James laughed. 'If you guys can handle the walk, I really think we should get back to the lodge. It's not so far. They have Carlsberg Extra Cold on tap, and by now the Silver Tours lot will have finished, so the karaoke will be open.'

28

THE RING

THEY STUMBLED INTO THE LODGE, BEDRAGGLED AND tired, an hour later. Mildred immediately put out the call to Barry, who was fussing about upstairs, and the staff rushed to get the returnees and new arrivals settled. Both Phil and Mick were starving, as was Kirsten, who had skipped out on dinner to make her dramatic exit, but there was plenty left over from the buffet, which Demelza set to work heating while they all stood around the fire, warming up. As Mick and Phil produced the coupons Doreen had given them, Barry fussed about, then announced that the only free room was one of the executive suites on the third floor. Both were delighted, even more so when they learned about their famous neighbour, Phil having apparently received Ernest Lemond's latest DVD as a stocking gift last year.

And there were more surprises in store. Jessica had warmed to both Phil and Mick on the return to the lodge, with neither sharing the ferocious destructive insanity of her now-hopefully-behind-bars lodger. Kirsten seemed to have warmed even more to Mick, laughing at all of his jokes, digging him in the ribs a couple of times, even though walking beside him she looked like an elf accompanying a sumo wrestler. Jessica wondered what kind of awkward situation they would face upon arrival, but Ben, who was fervently waiting in reception with Mildred for their return, was immediately taken to find out, when a tightly worn Arsenal hat was removed to reveal shoulder-length blonde locks, that Phil was actually Philippa.

After dinner was over, Jessica asked Kirsten for another quiet word.

'Look, I just wanted to say I'm sorry again that I didn't trust you. Well, I couldn't believe you were a thief, but the evidence was there, and I just didn't stop to think. I'm so sorry.'

Kirsten gave her a shy smile. 'It's okay. I kind of went off at the deep end, didn't I?'

'I deserved it. You didn't need to run away, though.'

'I got a little hot under the collar, I think.'

'Maybe we both need to calm down. Anyway, I wanted to say that, when we return to Bristol after New Year, if you want a full-time position, it's yours. You know, full salary, not any of that trainee wage rubbish I have to pay you because of government regulations.'

Kirsten's face lit up. 'Really, Ms. Lemond? Do you mean it? Oh, yes!'

As she leapt forward to embrace Jessica in a fierce hug, Jessica caught James's eye. He was standing beside the fireplace, eating a slice of chocolate log, and gave her a bemused smile. Jessica could only do her best to shrug.

'One more thing,' Jessica said, as Kirsten finally pulled away. 'No more of this Ms. Lemond. If you do it again, I'll dock you a month's wages.'

Kirsten gave a sharp nod. 'Certainly. I'll try.'

As she hurried back to where Mick was talking a bored-looking Mildred through a recent three-nil Gunners victory over Chelsea, James sauntered over.

'So, disaster averted,' he said. 'One last question and then I'd better get outside with a shovel and do my manly duty in the car park. Have you figured out who the thief really is? I imagine Barry would like to know who's been munching their way through the stock.'

'I think so,' Jessica said. 'I have something I need to make sure of first.'

Grandpa was upstairs in his suite, watching TV while Charity held a warm cloth over his knees. 'He's feeling a little bit arthritic,' she said, as Jessica entered.

'I can take over for a bit,' Jessica said, giving Charity a wink.

'Don't press too hard, love,' Grandpa said, as Jessica sat down in front of him and laid the warm cloth against his knees. 'It aches a little, but it'll be all right in the morning. The doctor has advised me against aspirin, unfortunately. Doesn't think my blood should get any thinner or my heart might give out. Problem is, I want to ride the log tomorrow.'

'Ride what log?'

'The Yule Log. We have the big ceremonial tree cutting in the morning. Apparently, it's a tradition that someone climbs the tree and sits at the top when it comes down, then rides it back to the place of burning.'

Jessica laughed. 'You're out of your mind.'

'Oh, I went out of that years ago. How are you, dear?'

'I'm fine.' She thought about her upcoming visit to

James's reindeer farm. 'Better than fine, actually. Very well.'

'I'm glad to hear it. I'm sorry I haven't been around as much to talk to you as I'd like. It's just the schedule, and you know, I've got to get things done before I sign out for the last time.'

'It's all right. I did have a question, though. Two, actually. You know, before you take the information to the grave.'

'Fire away.'

'Do you remember back in the fifties, you were in a movie called *Double Trouble*?'

Grandpa laughed. 'How could I forget? Wonderful time, being on a movie set. All those silly stunts we had to do. So much more fun than stand-up comedy, but you know, once you get typecast….'

'Do you remember the twins you worked with?'

Grandpa's eyes twinkled. 'Of course. Quite the pair of lookers, they were. Oh, those were the days….'

'Well, I, um, read on an, um, trivia website that you dated both. I just, ah, wondered, which one did you think you were dating?'

Grandpa smiled. 'Theodora and Trixie. A wonderful pair of ladies. We had such a grand time. However, I was such a terrible player in those days. All I really wanted was a chance with their sister.'

'Ellen? Really?'

Grandpa nodded. 'Things were different in those days, weren't they? I dated both, hoping one of them might bring their sister along as a chaperone. Oh, I was such a rogue. But they never did, and then filming wrapped, and I was back in Europe on a concert tour. I wonder what happened to those three? Long in their graves by now, I expect. As I ought to be.'

'Ah, they're downstairs. They own this lodge.'

Grandpa's jaw dropped, and Jessica wondered whether she ought to lay off the shocks a little. Then he said, 'Well, I'll never. Nice to know an old man can still be surprised. All of them? I'd better get down there before it's too late. I need to apologise to Theodora and Trixie, then get a ring on Ellen's finger.'

'Talking of rings … weren't you planning to propose to Charity?'

Grandpa stared at her for a moment then gave a cackling laugh. 'Heavens, no. What do you think I am, a cradle robber?'

'You said in your postcards to Dad that you were thinking about it.'

Grandpa laughed. 'I was spinning the boy a line, keeping him on his toes. But if I was, I would learn from previous mistakes and go for someone a little closer to my own age. Poor Charity's young enough to be my granddaughter.' With a cheeky grin, he added, 'At a push. I enjoy the company, but I'd never want to subject a girl as lovely as her to looking after an old dinosaur like me.'

'But she found a ring….'

Grandpa lifted an eyebrow. 'Did she now? That's the first I've heard about it.'

Jessica stood up. She had seen Charity taking a bottle of polish out of a drawer near the door, so she went over and opened it. A little ring box sat beside an unopened packet of dusters.

'Here,' she said, bringing it over. 'She said you left it where she would find it.'

Grandpa frowned. 'I did nothing of the sort. Open that up, will you?'

Jessica lifted the lid to reveal a beautifully ornate diamond ring. While she knew little about jewelry, even an untrained eye would know it was worth several thousand pounds.

Grandpa stared at it. 'Where on earth could that have possibly come from?'

'What is it? Is it something special?'

Then, just when Jessica had begun to believe she was beyond being shocked, a single tear rolled down Grandpa's cheek.

'Huh,' he said, giving a little shake of his head. 'There's another story attached to that one, that's for sure. The story that once … I had hoped might end all stories.'

29

CAPTURED

JESSICA FOUND THE THREE SISTERS TOGETHER AT A TABLE near the fire, enjoying breakfast.

'Good morning,' she said, pulling up a spare chair. 'How's the food today?'

'Fantastic as always,' Theodora said, as the other two mumbled their approval around mouthfuls of French toast. 'Honestly, I think I'm going to rot my false teeth with food as rich as this.'

'There's a reason we headhunted dear Demelza,' Trixie added. 'She was my favorite chef when I visited London on business. She wasn't cheap, but she was worth every penny.'

Jessica had already eaten two of the Swiss-style waffles on this morning's buffet and could certainly agree. Her stomach was satisfied but she was wondering if she could fit in one more. After all, it was set to be another busy day.

'I spoke to Grandpa at last,' she said.

Theodora lifted an ancient grey eyebrow. 'Oh? Did he remember us?'

'He certainly did.' She considered what she ought to

tell them. After all, the right information might make this lodge hers.

'And?'

'He told me he remembers all of you with the same fondness. All three of you. And he said it would be his absolute pleasure if you would allow him to join you for breakfast.' She gave a little smile as she looked up at Grandpa, hobbling across the room on a walking stick. 'In order that you might grill him for yourselves.'

'Oh, well, I suppose that would be nice....'

'Good morning, Grandpa,' Jessica said, as she stood up to free her seat, then helped him to sit down. 'Is there anything you'd like me to get you from the buffet?'

Grandpa looked at the three old ladies leaning forward in their wheelchairs and nodded. 'They serving scotch yet? I'm going to need a bit of courage for this.'

Jessica shook her head. 'Unfortunately not. I can get you some tea, though. With lemon?'

Grandpa and the three old ladies began to cackle. 'You know me, dear,' Grandpa said.

'How about I get you a communal plate of mince pies? They have low cholesterol ones that Demelza made for the Silver Tours group.'

Grandpa shook his head. 'Full fat, please. If we're going out, we might as well go out in style. Isn't that right, ladies?'

There were murmurs of agreement. Jessica caught Grandpa's eye, and he gave her a little wink.

She found Kirsten in the movie room, watching an early morning showing of *A Christmas Carol* with Mick.

'And they changed this bit from the book,' Kirsten was saying. 'He actually had a sister.'

'In the 1904 edit,' Mick said. 'Not in the original.'

'Are you sure?'

'I have a copy of the text on my phone. Give me a minute.'

Jessica patted Kirsten on the shoulder. 'Good morning,' she said.

'Oh, Ms … Jessica. How are you? Sorry again about last night.'

'No problem. Hi, Mick.'

Mick raised a chubby hand which was clutching an iPhone encased in an Arsenal cover. 'Good morning, Jessica. This is a wonderful place, isn't it? I hear they're opening up the ice rink this afternoon. I've always wanted to try.'

Jessica could hardly believe how normal Mick and Phil were outside of Doreen's influence. She smiled. 'I'm glad you're enjoying your stay. It's a, um, shame Doreen couldn't make it.'

Mick gave a smile that could have meant anything. 'I don't think we'll be seeing her,' he said. 'It turned out she was breaking a location order after an incident last year. She wasn't supposed to leave Gloucestershire. I picked up a text this morning which said she's being sent back to Bristol to be held on remand.'

If Father Christmas had suddenly jumped out of the TV and begun to dance, Jessica wouldn't have been happier. She tried not to smile too much as she nodded. 'Oh, that's too bad.'

'She was a bit of a nightmare, wasn't she?'

'You could say that,' Mick said. 'By the way, I'll pay for any damage that was caused to your flat.'

Jessica smiled. 'I appreciate it. By the way, where's Phil this morning?'

'She's gone snowboarding with Ben. He had the morning off.'

'Nice. Glad things are working out. If you still need a place to stay when we get back to Bristol, you can have Doreen's room,' Jessica said. 'Assuming she gets a good, long sentence and I can get a restraining order.'

'Thanks,' Mick said. Then, glancing at Kirsten, he added, 'I think I've already found a place to stay. I appreciate the offer though.'

Somewhat stunned by how quickly Kirsten's love life was developing, Jessica decided not to bother them further. Instead, she went looking for James. She found him outside with Mr. Dawes, clearing snow from the paths heading into the forest. Nearly thirty centimetres had fallen overnight in the end, and where the wind had caught it, the snow had drifted much deeper.

'Good morning,' he greeted her with a smile.

'Hi.' She felt that little tingle across her skin again, but ignored it. 'I was wondering how soon you needed to go back to your farm. I wondered if you could help me with something first.'

James grimaced. 'I need to get going soon,' he said. 'Can't you come?'

Jessica really, really wanted to go, but she shook her head. 'I have something I have to do. I have to flush out a pesky mouse. I was hoping you'd help me.'

'Later, maybe … if you still haven't caught it.'

'Sure.'

Mr. Dawes stood his shovel up in the snow with a grunt. 'I'll help you, lass,' he said. 'If you give me half an hour of shoveling first.'

'Sure.'

It was just after nine o'clock when Jessica and Mr. Dawes began their search for the little mouse which had been stealing from the lodge's food stores. They started at the top of the building on the south wing and made their way down, checking every empty room, closet, and store cupboard as they went. In two places—a closet in one of the unused executive suites and a broom cupboard on the second floor—they found evidence of someone hiding out, a couple of food wrappers here, a well-thumbed paperback there.

By the time they had made it down to the basement levels, they were still yet to discover the mysterious thief. They checked the first den Jessica had found, but it remained abandoned. Down in the staff car park, Jessica looked around.

'Are there no off-site buildings we could check?'

Mr. Dawes shook his head. 'I walked the sleigh run this morning. No tracks, no one in any of the stations. There's a couple of storage cupboards up by the ski lift, but you'd freeze to death. It's a real mystery, ain't it?'

Jessica looked around the parked cars. She tried the doors on a couple, but they were all locked. Then, like a cloud with a silver lining passing overhead, she had a sudden epiphany.

In the corner, parked near to the wall, was her Tomahawk motorbike.

With Mr. Dawes trailing behind her, she walked up to it, reached down and gave the awning covering the sidecar a tap.

'The game's up,' she said. 'Come on out. Don't worry, it's Christmas. We'll be lenient.'

At first she thought she was mistaken. Then, through

the awning something shifted. A zip slid up, and the awning lifted back.

He was sitting in the sidecar with a thick blanket wrapped around him, a paperback held in his gloved hands, and a paper cup of hot chocolate in a cup holder. A Christmas hat was perched on his head. As Jessica had thought, disguised as a member of staff, he had probably moved around the hotel from time to time without drawing attention.

'The mystery solved,' Jessica said. 'Come on, get out of there and let's get you upstairs before you freeze to death.'

With a grimace, the man stood up. 'Busted,' Dick Burd said.

30

JUSTICE AND REVELATIONS

'THE MAN IS A CRIMINAL!' BARRY SHOUTED, STOMPING back and forth in front of Jessica and Dick Burd, who stood with his head lowered like a defendant at a court hearing. 'He should be behind bars!'

'Come on, show a little Christmas spirit,' Jessica said. 'I mean, hasn't he suffered enough? He's been hiding out in the basements, surviving off scraps of food and chocolate bars—which he has promised to pay for. I know it's not right, but he's sorry.'

'I'm sorry,' Dick muttered.

'We are not a charity organisation,' Barry said. 'We are a hotel, and this man not only broke in, but he has been stealing goods from our stocks.'

'I walked in through the front door,' Dick said. 'And those chocolate bars were actually out of date. Everything else I took came from the kitchen bin.'

Barry turned on his heels, glared at Dick—who had wisely lowered his head again—and stamped his foot. 'I—don't—care. You are a thief and a trespasser, and you should be in prison with the rest of the criminals.'

'I'm a private detective,' Dick said.

'Don't talk back to me! As soon as the police arrive, you'll be in cuffs.'

'We're snowed in,' Jessica said. 'The police won't be able to get here for a couple of days. Come on, it's Christmas!'

'I don't—'

The door opened. James came in then stood aside, holding the door open for a wheelchair to pass through.

'What is the meaning of this interruption?' Barry snapped, stamping his foot again. 'We're in the middle of a private staff meeting—'

'Hush, little one,' Theodora said, as Mildred wheeled her through the door. The receptionist handed the chair to James, gave him a quick smirk, then hurried out, closing the door with a smart thump. James wheeled Theodora up alongside Jessica and Dick. He gave Jessica's hand a surreptitious squeeze, then followed Mildred out.

Barry was staring at Theodora. 'What … did you just say?'

'Remember me, now, do you? Hush, little Barry, close your eyes, listen to my lullaby. Time for quiet, time for sleep, time to watch the reindeer leap….'

'You,' he said.

'I used to visit you in the orphanage,' she said. 'I used to sing you to sleep all the time. I don't have the voice for it now, but I was quite the singer back in my day. And you were a lovely little boy, even with all the bluster. After the start you had, I'm so glad you grew up into a responsible human being.'

'I—I—I—'

Jessica didn't think she'd ever seen Barry speechless, but it was quite a sight. His hair jumped with every attempt to articulate, like an old car trying to start.

'I've looked after you all these years,' Theodora said. 'And you looked after me. Well, my property.'

'Your…?'

'This lodge belongs to me and my sisters. What you like to call the conglomerate. We never felt the need to reveal ourselves until now, preferring to stay in the background while you ran things expertly. However, I can't let you punish this young man unjustly. Yes, he has trespassed and stolen, but no doubt he had his reasons. There will be time to hear them, but first I'd like to extend a welcome to him here at our lodge. After all, you say we aren't a charity and you are correct, but we are chari*table*, and there is no better time to be charitable than at Christmas.'

'He can't be allowed to get off scot free!'

'And he won't. Jessica dear, please explain.'

'I need someone to cut and sand wood,' she said. 'A lot of it. It's a tough job, and it'll take a couple of days. For all Mr. Dawes's enthusiasm, I can't put the job on an old man like him, not to mention his other duties.' She gave Dick a nudge in the ribs. 'A strong chap like this will be just the ticket.'

Barry's face had gone blank. His eyes moved from Theodora to Jessica to Dick, then back again. Finally his mouth opened.

'And the car park needs shoveling,' he said in a hollow, defeated voice. 'Every morning.'

'Then the sentence is served,' Theodora said. 'Jessica dear, you may escort this young man to his place of work.'

'Come on,' Jessica said to Dick. 'Let's go.'

As she led Dick to the door, she heard Theodora's voice behind her: 'Were you really selling out-of-date chocolate bars? We could get sued if someone gets sick, you know.'

'They weren't for sale. That's why they were in the stock room.'

'Then why didn't you just throw them away…?'

∿

Dick Burd, chastened, proved to be a good worker. With Mr. Dawes helping to supervise, they quickly got through Jessica's wood cutting and sanding tasks. By the end of the second day, they were ready to test the wooden skates they had made.

Grandpa volunteered to be the test dummy. Somewhat disappointed that the felling of the Yule Tree had been put off for a few days because of the excessive snowfall, he needed a new challenge. Having painstakingly cleared the snow off the frozen lake, Jessica helped the old man down to the lakeside while Dick Burd carried a wheelchair with a pair of makeshift skates fitted to its wheels.

Mr. Dawes, who had worked so hard to prepare the lake, took the honour of pushing Grandpa around. Jessica and Dick watched from the bench outside the changing rooms as they made a couple of ungainly circuits of the central tree.

'So, when are you going to ask him?' Jessica asked at last. Dick had said little while in her company, performing his penal tasks without complaint, only speaking when he needed to ask for direction.

'Ask him what?'

'About whether he murdered Mavis.'

'Oh, that.'

'That's why you're here, isn't it?'

Dick said nothing. He stared out at the lake for a long time, watching Grandpa whooping and yelling as Mr. Dawes spun the wheelchair around.

'Dick?'

He didn't look at her. Jessica watched his expression carefully. The boldness she had seen when he confronted her at her parents' house had vanished, and she wondered if it had ever been anything more than an act. She remembered how they had seen him helping people on the way here. Perhaps she had him all wrong.

'You're not here for that, are you?'

Very slowly, Dick shook his head. 'That was just a cover,' he said. 'I read about her death in the newspaper and I volunteered my services. However, it didn't take long to realise there was no real evidence against Ernest Lemond whatsoever.'

'Then what? Wait a minute. That ring … you didn't have something to do with that, did you?'

Dick sighed, then lifted a hand and unzipped his jacket. He reached inside and pulled out a little leather case. Opening it, he handed it to Jessica. Inside was a black and white picture of a pretty woman posing with a young girl in front of a set of swings.

'My mother and grandmother,' he said. 'Ernest Lemond is my grandfather, but I don't think he knows it.'

'What?'

'My grandmother's name was Audrey Lane,' Dick said, so quietly Jessica had to lean closer to hear. 'She worked on a US state network television channel as a boom operator. He gave her that ring and proposed to her.'

'They were married?'

Dick shook his head. 'My grandmother died when my mother was a teenager. I never met her. The way my mother told it was that shortly after Ernest proposed, he had to go back to England on urgent business. My grandmother never saw or heard from him again. He never knew she was pregnant. She wrote him letters, but all she had was the address of a TV network. She never received a reply.'

'Then, that ring—'

'I wanted him to find it. I wanted him to remember her. I planned to give it to him myself, but I chickened out.'

Jessica remembered Grandpa's reaction to the ring when she had opened the box. She explained to Dick. 'If what you're saying is true, then that would make us … cousins?'

For the first time she could remember, Dick smiled. 'Something like that,' he said. 'I'm very pleased to meet you.'

'And me to meet you. And, knowing him the way I do, I'm pretty sure Grandpa would be pleased to meet you too. After the life he's had, I'm not sure anything would surprise him.'

Mr. Dawes, with Muffin curled up on his lap as they sat around a table in the Victorian café an hour later, having picked up a lift on a sleigh as James took it for a test ride, could hardly contain his laughter. Beside him, neither Grandpa nor Dick was laughing, while James had made his excuses to go outside and check over the sleigh. Jessica half wished she had taken up his offer, even though the story Grandpa had related to Dick topped any of the excitement she had experienced so far during her stay at Snowflake Lodge.

'I spent my whole life trying to replace her,' Grandpa said. 'You know how everyone has their perfect match out there somewhere, but so few people ever find them? She was mine, was Audrey. Oh, she was an oil painting, and boy, this picture, it takes me back. I don't have many regrets, but that's one. Audrey. Oh, Audrey.'

Dick, much to Jessica's surprise, gave him a pat on the back. Beside them, Mr. Dawes continued to chuckle.

'And there's me with the sheltered life,' he said. 'Wouldn't change it, hearing all this. Nothing like a bit of peace and quiet, is there?'

'I fell for her hook, line, and sinker,' Grandpa said. 'I gave her that ring because she was the woman I intended to spend the rest of my life with. It cost me a bloody fortune, but it was worth every penny. No chance I was ever letting her get away, but I did, didn't I?'

'What happened?' Jessica asked.

'It was a typical rich man, poor man thing. I met her while I was working on a TV show in the US, but I had a tour booked. I planned to finish the tour then go back to Audrey and make an honest woman of her. But my management talked me out of it. Told me I needed a celebrity marriage to push my career. I wasn't having it, of course, but then I got the letter.'

'What letter?'

I received a letter from Audrey, telling me she no longer wanted to marry me. She had found someone else, and that was that.'

Dick shook his head. 'She loved you until the day she died, my mother always said. She tried so many times to write to you, but she never got a reply.'

'I only ever got the one letter.'

'At the TV station?'

'No, in those days I was working all over the place. It was addressed to my flat in London.'

'She didn't know your address. It couldn't have been from her.'

Ernest looked up and sighed. 'You know, now that you

say it, you're telling me what I always believed. I was just too naïve to follow up on it. My management would do anything to keep me on their path, because in those days they were earning as much from my contracts as I was. I didn't figure it out until much later.'

Jessica didn't know what to say. On the one hand it was a terrible case of unrequited love which had been passed over, but on the other it was better late than never.

Grandpa reached for the photograph again. 'And this … this lady is your mother?'

'Elaine.'

Grandpa nodded. 'My daughter. Is she…?'

'I'm afraid she passed a few years ago.'

'She never tried to contact me?'

'I think she planned to one day, but she never got around to it. Her death was sudden. She had a heart attack while she was walking her dog.'

'It's all terribly sad.'

'She loved you, though. We both did. We had all your DVDs.'

Grandpa gave a tired shrug. 'It's not the same, is it?'

'And you were an inspiration for my career.'

Grandpa frowned. 'Jessica said you were a private investigator?'

Dick shook his head, then gave Jessica a little smile. 'Not at all,' he said. 'I'm pleased to know I had you fooled. I'm a method actor. I've appeared in a few West End shows, and even had a bit part last year on *Eastenders*.' He smiled. 'I was "boy-in-background-on-a-moped".'

Grandpa gave a long sigh. 'Following in your grandfather's footsteps. Well, that's something at least.'

'With your permission, I'd like to tell everyone that I'm your grandson in an effort to further my career.'

Grandpa burst into laughter. 'Nothing would please me

more. Let's make sure we get a photograph just so people can see the resemblance. Jessica, do you have a phone?'

'I'm afraid I dropped it in the hot spring.'

'Oh. Mr. Dawes?'

Mr. Dawes shook his head, scooped up Muffin and deposited her on the tabletop where she nosed disinterestedly at a plate of marshmallows. 'Not got nothing modern but there's the old antique Polaroid on the stand over there. Will waive the fiver fee we usually charge the customers since we can treat it as a tester.'

Jessica turned to follow his gaze and saw an ancient wooden camera on a stand which she had assumed was part of the café's decoration.

'Does that thing actually work?'

'It did last year, so I imagine it'll be all right. Built stuff to last in those days, people did.'

31

MERRY CHRISTMAS

THE DAYS PASSED GENTLY, WITH CHRISTMAS approaching like a vintage steam train out of the fog. Grandpa, determined to live the remainder of his life to the full, managed to cajole Dick into accompanying him, under the guise of family bonding. More often than not, when Jessica went looking for him, she was told they had gone snow-biking, cross-country skiing, or, even on one terrifying occasion where it turned out Grandpa was a mere onlooker, ice lake swimming.

The Yule Tree was felled without incident, with Grandpa thankfully being talked out of perching in the upper branches, that honour being bestowed upon an unfortunate teddy bear which was luckily caught by one of the Silver Tours group as it bounced out of the tree upon felling. In the days after, after dinner each evening, a section of the tree was burned in an open fire on the front patio, with assembled guests using its heat to roast marshmallows while the sound of Christmas songs filled the evening air.

Jessica, still on duty, but having fixed most of the

lodge's damaged piping using old replacements she had found in a store room beside the car park, and with little to do other than shovel snow, began to feel a little left out. Kirsten spent most of her time with Mick, Ben and Phil were a proper item, and there was even a rumour that Barry had asked Mildred for a date after a drunken night at karaoke, and that Mildred, having at first refused, had agreed to be taken for dinner somewhere in Inverness over the New Year, providing that Christmas hats weren't a required item of dress. When Jessica saw them together, there was certainly an awkwardness between them that she hadn't seen before, but on one occasion she even heard Barry whistling, and that had to be a good thing.

She was sitting in the dining room one evening, contemplating the event she had planned for tomorrow—the first skating trip for the Silver Tours group, including a sleigh ride, a meeting with Santa at the Grotto, followed by lunch at the Victorian café—when Theodora came wheeling over.

'Jessica, dear, there you are. I've been trying to track you down for days.'

'Sorry, I was just busy getting things ready for Christmas.'

'I wanted to tell you, your grandfather explained everything to us. I know you knew the truth and didn't say, but we've been around as long as many trees, we can handle it.' She chuckled. 'Wow, that old dog. What a player he was. He must have lived enough for ten people.'

Jessica smiled. 'Rather him than me.'

'I wanted to let you know that the offer still stands. About the lodge.'

Jessica felt a tingle of excitement. 'The lodge?'

'And its grounds. The ski run, the old train line, the lake, the hot spring. Everything. We're old now, and we can't run it like we used to. We have plenty of money. We'd like to slip quietly into the background knowing it was in good hands.'

Jessica nodded. 'I understand. And I think your offer is too good to be true.'

'So you'll accept?'

Jessica sighed. Then, with a wistful smile, she shook her head. 'I'm very sorry but I can't. I spent my whole childhood growing up in the shadow of two people who never had to work a day in their lives. Don't get me wrong, I love my parents and they're not bad people, they've just never known what it feels like to work hard for what you have … and the satisfaction you feel when you achieve it.'

'You're turning down the offer of a multi-million pound property?'

'Yes, I am.'

Theodora looked at her for a long time. Then, her old mouth wrinkled into a smile, and she reached up to pat Jessica's cheek with a leathery palm.

'A lot of things have impressed me over the years, dear, but none more than you. I'm certain your grandfather—and your parents in their way—are very proud of you.'

'My grandfather earned every penny of his fortune,' Jessica said. 'I like to think that I'm capable of earning every penny of mine.' She reached out to pat Theodora's hand. 'However … I do have some suggestions for the lodge, if you don't mind.'

'I'd love to hear them.'

'I think you could do worse than giving ownership or at least custodianship of this lodge to Barry … and Mildred. And Mr. Dawes, and all the others from disadvantaged backgrounds whom you've brought here to work over the years. And I would like to see it continue in the same vein. School groups, particularly from low income areas or special needs institutions … you have to share the magic of a place like this. And not just in the winter, but in the summer too. Expand the conservation projects and the nature schemes that were mentioned on the website … give a chance to people who don't have one to experience a different way of life.'

'Can you write all this down for me?'

Jessica, snapping her mouth shut to stop her words falling over themselves, nodded. 'I've already made some notes. And if it's okay by you, for a couple of months of the year at least, I'd like to come up here and work. Lead the tours, teach disadvantaged kids how to ski, once I've got the hang of it myself, of course. And as soon as Kirsten's experienced enough to manage my business in Bristol, I'd like to consider a full-time position.'

Theodora smiled and patted her on the cheek again. 'That would be most acceptable,' she said. 'I'd be delighted to have you around. Until I plop my clogs at least.'

The skating excursion was a huge success. So much so that the head of the Silver Tours group requested that another trip be planned for after Christmas. Seeing the thrilled old-timers sliding about the ice and hearing their whoops of delight was something Jessica hadn't expected to find so satisfying.

Sitting beside her on the bench while a group of volunteers on ice skates spun the wheelchairs around, Mr. Dawes gave her a knowing grin.

'Makes you happy, don't it?' he said. 'That's what Christmas is all about.'

Jessica nodded. She wanted to say something, but she had a sudden lump in her throat, and anything she did say would have come out partially sobbed. So she just smiled and stayed quiet.

～

The morning of Christmas Eve, she was ready for a couple of days of rest when James found her in the dining room.

'You're not busy, are you?' he said, flashing her a wink. 'I need an elf.'

'What?'

'Don't worry, Barry's got a costume. He was going to do it, but I talked him out of it.'

'What for?'

'I have to go and get the children's group from the Edinburgh orphanage. Their train arrives in forty-five minutes. We like to pick them up in style.'

'And, um, you'll be wearing…?'

'I'll be an elf too, of course. The big man doesn't appear until tomorrow. We're just underlings.'

The thought of seeing James in an elf costume thrilled Jessica more than perhaps it should have. She laughed. 'Go on, then. Why not?'

Twenty minutes later, James emerged from behind a screen dressed in a skintight forest green elf costume, with a little pointed hat perched on his head. Jessica covered her mouth as she tried not to laugh, while at the same time feeling frustrated at how impressed she felt with the way the muscles on his shoulders and legs stretched against the material.

'We'll put ski jackets on until we're in sight of the station,' he said, cheeks flushed. 'Otherwise we'll freeze to death.'

'It's fetching,' she said, covering her mouth. 'It definitely suits you.'

He held up a plastic bag. Something green glittered inside. 'Your turn.'

Outside, Mr. Dawes was keeping an eye on the six reindeer harnessed to the sleigh. Other staff and guests clapped and cheered as James and Jessica made their way through the lobby and out of the main doors. James, who had gotten over his initial embarrassment, waved and smiled at the crowd. Jessica, horrified by how tight the suit was, gave a shy wave as she hurried after him, out of the main doors and down the steps to where the sleigh was waiting.

'Let's go,' James said, climbing up to the driver's seat and helping Jessica up beside him. 'Are you ready?'

Jessica nodded.

'Yah!' he shouted, snapping the reins. Mr. Dawes stepped aside and the reindeer set off, bells jingling as the sleigh raced across the snowy car park.

Even though she had been staying at the lodge for more than three weeks, it was still her first time to ride on the sleigh, and she had her heart in her mouth as James expertly guided the reindeer around corners, the deer running far faster than she had expected. By the time they reached the main road—still blanketed with snow and impassable to regular traffic, she was just about able to enjoy it. And by the time they reached the nearest town twenty minutes later, she was about ready to label it the best form of transport ever.

Passersby, wrapped up against the cold, clapped and waved as they passed. James and Jessica waved back, responding to cries of 'Merry Christmas!' and posing where they could for photographs. A few minutes later they reached the little train station and pulled into a spot where a cone had a laminated sign taped to it which read, 'Reserved for reindeer parking'. As the station master pulled it out of the way, he called up to them, 'Ten minutes to the train. It's on time this morning.'

'That was epic,' Jessica said, as the reindeer settled. 'I've never experienced anything like it.'

'Just think how those kids are going to feel,' James said. 'That's what it's all about, isn't it?'

Jessica nodded. 'It is.'

There was a short pause, then James said, 'You know, I heard you were planning to come up here and work. Mr. Dawes told me.'

Jessica felt her cheeks glowing again. She had wanted to tell James about her decision, but there had never felt like a right moment. Whenever she saw him it was for something related to work.

'I thought it might be fun,' she said.

'I'm, um, happy to hear it.'

'It had nothing to do with you,' Jessica blurted, immediately feeling like an idiot, and then realising at the same time that in a small way, it did.

'Of course not,' James said quickly, looking away, idling tugging at the reins. 'I wouldn't want you to do anything because of me. But … if you did … I wouldn't mind.'

Jessica nodded. She glanced at him, caught his eye, then quickly looked away. 'I wouldn't mind either,' she said, but instead of words, all that came out was a dry croak.

'You know, I heard Barry was taking Mildred out somewhere in Inverness. There are a couple of nice restaurants there.'

Jessica wanted to say something witty about Nessie steaks, but she definitely hadn't inherited her grandfather's way with words. Instead, all she said was, 'That sounds nice.'

They both looked at each other and nodded. Jessica felt

something press against her hand where it lay on the bench, and she looked down to see that James's glove had closed the gap, and the outside of his glove was pressing against the outside of hers. It felt hopelessly romantic.

A train horn blared. Both jumped, nearly head-butting each other.

'That's the train,' James said.

'I know it is,' Jessica said.

'It's coming.'

'I know.'

'So, it's a date?'

'What?'

'Inverness?'

Jessica met his eyes. 'Yes,' she said.

'Good.'

The train horn blared again as it pulled into the station. Moments later a crowd of children began pushing through the exit gates, ignoring the shouts of a teacher to be orderly.

'No way!'

'Cool!'

'Wow!'

Jessica glanced at James again. He was watching the children with a small, satisfied smile on his face. 'Merry Christmas,' she whispered.

James didn't look at her, but his hand closed over hers and gave a gentle squeeze.

'Merry Christmas, Jessica,' he said.

ACKNOWLEDGMENTS

More thanks goes to my fantastic cover designer, Elizabeth Mackey, Lisa Lee for the proofreading, and also to my eternal muses Jenny Twist and John Daulton.

Lastly, but certainly not least, many thanks goes to my wonderful Patreon supporters:

Alan McDonald
Anja Peerdeman
Amaranth Dawe
Betty Martin
Elizabeth Pennington
Gail Beth La Vine
Jane Ornelas
Janet Hodgson
Jenny Brown
Katherine Crispin
Ken Gladwin
Leigh McEwan
Nancy
Ron

Rosemary Kenny
Sharon Kenneson

You guys are fantastic and your support means so much.

Happy reading,
    CW
    April, 2021

For more information:
www.amillionmilesfromanywhere.net

ABOUT THE AUTHOR

CP Ward is a pen name of Chris Ward, the author of the dystopian *Tube Riders* series, the horror/science fiction *Tales of Crow* series, and the *Endinfinium* YA fantasy series, as well as numerous other well-received stand alone novels.

Christmas at Snowflake Lodge is Chris's fifth Christmas book.

There will be more …

Chris would love to hear from you:
www.amillionmilesfromanywhere.net
chrisward@amillionmilesfromanywhere.net

Printed in Great Britain
by Amazon

CHRISTMAS AT SNOWFLAKE LODGE

CP WARD

CHRISTMAS AT SNOWFLAKE LODGE